I0714665

# THE GHOSTS OF BOHEMIAN GROVE
## KEVIN ALLARDICE

Spuyten Duyvil

New York City

ISBN 978-1-956005-67-7

Library of Congress Cataloging-in-Publication Data

Names: Allardice, Kevin, author.
Title: The ghosts of Bohemian Grove / Kevin Allardice.
Description: New York City : Spuyten Duyvil, [2022]
Identifiers: LCCN 2022030162 | ISBN 9781956005677 (paperback)
Subjects: LCGFT: Novels.
Classification: LCC PS3601.L4149 G49 2022 |
DDC 813/.6--dc23/eng/20220624
LC record available at https://lccn.loc.gov/2022030162

# One.

Midway upon the journey of our life I found myself within a forest dark, for the straightforward pathway had been lost.

More specifically, I was somewhere in, or near, Monte Rio, California, a small town—or rather a census-designated place—on the Russian River, a couple hours north of San Francisco. Once known as Vacation Wonderland, the census-designated place in the redwoods still had that moniker slung over its main drag in green, san-seriffed letters, beyond which people languidly floated down the river, their inner-tubes leashed to bouied coolers of Natural Lite. Those vacationers, whose pink bellies looked melanomic from the sun, seemed like central casting extras just there to remind me that I wasn't in Guerneville. Guerneville was the town just up the road and had a hip, vibrant culture. Geographically, Monte Rio was only a few miles from Guerneville, but culturally, it was light years away; Monte Rio's economy seemed shaped more by the meth trade than by wine tastings. But there I was.

"There" was an artists' retreat at which I had been ecstatic to receive a week-long stay at the end of 2018. As a writer, I was still sheepish about fitting myself under the umbrella-term "artist," but when I arrived at the retreat, I quickly realized—pulling up to a small house poised precariously on a steep, winding mountain road, that precarity echoing in the groan of my emergency brake as it strained to keep my car sedentary—that this was simply a man's house with a spare guest room. The man in question was standing on his porch, clad in Crocs and wispy shirt sleeves, watering a potted something.

When I walked up, he said, "Help you?"

"I'm Kevin Allardice. I'm here for the retreat."

"You're Kevin?" His hose was now overflowing what looked to be a twig stuck into dirt.

"I am." I extended my hand for a shake.

"With a name like that, I was expecting a woman."

My room shared a wall with his. There was a desk and a double bed. On the desk was a Post-It with the wifi password: *wifi_password2*. Across the hall was the one bathroom, but just as I set my bag down on the bed, my host came in with an empty salad bowl.

"Just in case you don't want to make the trip across the hall in the middle of the night."

"You mean like a bedpan?"

"So what kind of stuff you write?"

"You saw my application, right?"

"I'm a busy man." He set the salad bowl beside my bed. "Was it like your parents thought they were having a girl and so they settled on 'Kevin,' but then had a surprise boy and just kept the name?"

"About the food, I have some dietary restrictions. I mentioned them on my application, but."

"I'm told I snore."

That evening, as I was unpacking my clothes into a closet about as roomy as an upright coffin—filling it with shirts and shorts I hadn't worn in years, if ever, but which I'd somehow thought I'd warm to during this week of writerly indulgence, as if given enough time, I'd suddenly become the sort of person who was not deeply ashamed of his pale, squishy calves—I noticed something: words gouged into the interior of the closet. I grabbed the Post-It from the desk, placed it over the etched phrase and, with a nubby pencil from my bag, shaded over the words until I saw: *Illegitimi non carborundum.*

Later that night, after I could not bring myself to make water in the salad bowl—though I tried, achingly—I ventured out of my room. The bathroom door was closed. I put my hand on the knob and found it locked. I assumed my host was using the facilities himself, until I heard, coming from his bedroom, a snore like a slowly malfunctioning accordion. So I took my full bladder outside, where in the cool mountain air I was able to relax enough to micturate into the waist-high weeds, during which I felt a flare-up of atavistic pride in the audacity of my outdoorsy self. A real Jeremiah Johnson, I was, the steam from my piss rising into the night air like the smoke of some ritualistic effigy. Then I went back to bed and played a game on my cell-phone that involved matching up pieces of candy, until I fell asleep.

By the third night—between days spent downloading more candy-related games on my cell-phone and not writing—of having to pee outside (the bathroom door only seemed locked after dark), a mosquito bite had appeared near the base of my penis and the novelty of being outdoorsy had worn off.

After zipping up, I walked down to the river. The moonlight fluttering on the surface of the water made me think of Bob Ross, whose painting show I'd often watch as a child to fall asleep. Somehow what was relaxing about this scene was the memory of its painted simulacrum rather than the thing itself, but I still enjoyed it enough to stroll along the pebbly bank for a while. I've always preferred pebbly or even rocky shores to sandy ones. I'm a firm believer that nature should come in pieces sizable enough to not be abrasive between one's toes. Around me, in the mountains, owls were practicing their backing vocals for "Sympathy for the Devil," and the cars passing on the highway were so distant they might have actually been the sound of the breeze through the trees.

Then, there, just down the bank, I saw: a leopard, a lion, and a she-wolf, standing like sentries, and I nearly shit my pants. That is, my pajama bottoms. It wasn't until I noticed the Ray-Bans propped on top of the she-wolf's face that I realized these were ersatz beasts, molded in plastic and installed to scare off trespassers, human or other. I must have wandered onto private land. I figured I'd better get back before some possessive landowner saw my inky silhouette in the moonlight and grabbed his atlatl. Vacation Wonderland or no, this was still the part of California where you could be shotgunned for stumbling onto someone's single, spindly marijuana plant, the part of California where people draped the State of Jefferson flag on the back of their 4Runners.

Judging from the curve of the river that I'd followed, I figured I could cut across that patch of grass over there and find the main road that would lead me back to the retreat. As I proceeded through this shortcut, I found the crushed empties of more Natural Lites, a few deflated floaties, spent birdshot casings, some owl-pellets that upon closer inspection—as the sight of them fanfarred in my chest the sense of naturalist gusto I'd felt when dissecting owl-pellets in junior high—turned out to be small loaves of shit, perhaps of human provenance.

The main road was not showing itself. I kept walking, expecting it to be just over every rise or around every turn, but the road stubbornly did not appear. The river-reflected moonlight was now gone. And that is how, midway upon the journey of our life I found myself within a forest dark, for the straightforward pathway had been lost.

Fuck.

I stopped. I sat. The pebbles of the beach were gone; they'd given way to the granular, the stuff that I'd be shaking out of my slippers months from now, finding in the folds of my pajama bottoms long after multiple washes.

I heard the trickling sound of a nearby stream. I wasn't sure how far from the river I'd wandered, but I figured finding my way back to it was my best chance at reorienting myself. So I followed the trickle, through trees and bushes. The redwoods smelled dry and sweet. My slippered feet on the pine needles sounded like chewing. Things moved in my periphery that were either real or eyeball floaters.

I came to a small clearing and, upon seeing a human figure, momentarily thought I was having another cardiac event. I was supposed to be avoiding shocks to the heart, not subjecting it to further trauma. The man was facing away from me, clad in a white linen suit, which helped him attract and reflect the moonlight; he was leaning against a redwood, one hand bracing himself against the massive tree, the other presumably holding his pecker, as I soon realized that the trickling I'd heard was in fact the sound of this man pissing forcefully against the base of the tree.

(And to those readers who hope this motif of bodily fluids will abate—abandon all hope, ye who enter here.)

"Sorry," I said, "sorry," as was my training, the old Puritanism filtered down through generations of secular self-shaming. I often found myself nostalgic for the days when believing in a draconian god was a non-option; it would have given my pervasive anxiety and shame a focus or at least fulcrum, a theological purpose. As it was, I had no signal but I had the noise, and that noise always sounded like: "Sorry."

The man kept pissing.

I waited, humbled by the aggressiveness of his stream.

Finally—a rivulet making its way through the pine-nettled forest floor toward my feet—the man did a little hop-dance to mark the end of, and shake off the rest of, his pee. He zipped up and turned toward me.

"Well then," he said. "You appear lost."

"I am." I stepped aside to avoid the slowly approaching pee stream.

"Allow me to show you the way."

His suit jacket was buttoned most of the way up his chest, finally parting for the lapels just an inch beneath the little black budding of his bow tie. His graying eyebrows were architectural echoes of his mustache: flared out in ways that on any other face would lend a demonic menace, but which on his face seemed to aid a look of concerned interest. Perhaps this benevolence was the effect of his brow, which sloped at the edges of his eyes.

I said, "You know the retreat?"

"Sir, I helped found that place."

I followed as he parted branches. He was careful to not let them swing back and thwack me.

"Tell me," he said over his shoulder, "on which sort of crow's nest of power do you perch? Private or public? Or some nettled conduit betwixt the two? On what sort of lever does your paw rest? And how many people will die if you accidentally put weight upon that lever? I don't intend toward hostility. I ask with genuine curiosity."

"Um. I'm just a writer. I teach too, but not very well."

My ankle was itching and I was starting to worry I'd grazed poison oak. That mnemonic device about leaves of three, letting them be, which my wife had reminded me of before I drove up here, only made me see poisoned threes in everything; nature had its way of turning me into some numerological conspiracy theorist who scratched at his skin like there were meth-hallucinated spiders crawling around under there. But it was dark out, and I couldn't see the leaves anyway, so, without the ability to read the fibonacci sequence into the leafology of the forest, I had the mental space to replay in my mind what my guide here had just asked me.

"Wait, what?"

"Pardon?" he said, stopping, turning to me. "Did you say a writer?"

"Did you say crow's nest of power?"

"Delightful!" The moonlight was behind him, but I could just make out a smile beneath his mustache. "A writer! That's who we wanted here in the first place. Go 'head, ask J.C.—the club began as journalists. But now, well—maybe keep your avocation in your breast pocket around some of the more recent members. That's what I do. Believe me, seniority means nothing if one of these hotheads finds out I used to be a Hearst Boy." He grabbed my shoulders, gave a hearty squeeze, then turned and kept marching through the dark.

I asked, "You're a journalist?"

"No need to flatter me with feigned ignorance. I'm not as humble as you'd imagine. But my fiction is what precedes me. Even a century in death, I enjoy royalties on my invented stories more than my true ones."

The man's face was turned away from me, but the moonlit visage that I could recall from the clearing was one not so much hoary as decayed. There'd been a pallor beyond age. I stopped.

"My God."

He stopped, turned to me. "I said I had a healthy ego, but not that strong."

The mustache. The eyebrows. The outline of his writing career and American-colonial sartorial style. All wrapped in the specter of death. "Are you—" I hesitated, saw him leaning forward encouragingly. "Are you Mark Twain?"

His silhouette went bolt upright again. He took a long, measured breath. "I'd take that as a joke if you struck me as a funny fellow. Instead I will say, calmly and with the patience of a goddamn hourglass, that the man you refer to by unit of measurement, rather than by his Christian moniker, may have positioned himself quite successfully as a man of adventure, but does he have one of these?"

He opened his jacket with great flare.

"I can't see," I said. "It's really dark out here."

He stepped forward, grabbed my right hand and pulled it to his chest. Suddenly my hand was in a wet mess of squish. I thought of those gags in haunted houses: put your hand through this curtain and some moist grapes become eyeballs, a pile of al dente spaghetti becomes brains, the lack of visual confirmation turning the tactile world into the horrors of the abject. I wondered why my guide here had a pocket full of pudding, when he said, "Given to me by pirates off the coast of La Paz, before being tossed overboard. Mr. Clemens died snoozing in a wicker chair. I died feeling the sting of salt water in a machete wound. *Roughing It*, my keister."

I yanked my hand back, felt between my fingers the cold stick of blood that hadn't circulated for a century.

"My name," he said, buttoning his jacket back up, "is Ambrose Bierce."

"Oh, yeah. Of course. Sorry, I should have known, it's just—you know, dark out."

"You know my work, then."

I stopped myself from asking if he had any hand sanitizer, instead saying, "Is the river nearby? I'd like to wash my hands."

"We're almost to the front gates, Mr.—you didn't tell me your name, Mr. Writer."

"Kevin Allardice," I said.

"Isn't that a girl's name?"

"So you're saying I have to wait until we get back to wash my hands?"

"Onward."

I followed him through more forest, grasping for leaves—poisoned or not—to wipe my hand.

"Tell me, what of my works do you read most? I'm curious about what lasts the crucible of time."

After trying to wipe my hand clean, I now had a few twigs stuck in the gummy webbing between thumb and index finger. "Oh, you know, they're all good." I seemed to recall his name from an AP Lit anthology. "But, uh, you know 'Incident at Hanging Rock,' that one is, it's right up there."

He stopped again, but didn't turn to face me. "You could have said *Huckleberry Finn* if you really wanted to rub sand in my wound. But I believe you refer to 'An Occurrence at Owl Creek Bridge.' It's been turned into a film, you know, thricely."

"That's what I meant. Yes. I—I'm bad with titles, but yes. I fuckin' love that one. Really."

Ambrose did not move. Somewhere a wolf howled. As it continued, it betrayed itself as a human impression of a wolf howl.

"Wait," I said, "the front gates? There's no gate at the retreat."

"We're close."

"To what, though?"

"Why, we're going back to the Grove."

# Two.

The Bohemian Grove did, in fact, have front gates, and I made the mistake of walking through them. I did not, at the time, understand what that would mean, didn't understand the rules.

The gates were not ostentatious—no glowering gargoyles perched atop neoclassical crenelations, just modest wooden posts and a latticed yett that parted upon our approach without any visible human effort. We walked through and the path continued, meandering through the redwoods. I couldn't see where we were going but I could vaguely sense it, the penumbra of fireworks beyond the trees, the throb of music.

"Big party?" I asked.

"Our little perambulation meant we missed the Cremation of Care. The effigy, you can smell the smoldering."

"Effigy? Isn't the Fire Danger Rating like pretty high right now? I think I saw it was red on a sign when I was driving up here. And I know there's a Spare the Air Day coming up."

My guide looked at me, and his eyebrows twitched. "You're amusing."

"Thanks, Ambrose."

For some reason, saying his name jarred something loose: "Wait. Ambrose Bierce."

He stopped, perhaps thinking that I'd literally been telling him to wait.

"*The Devil's Dictionary*. Right?"

He smiled. The edges of his mustache flinched skyward. "You've got it now."

"I actually read that one."

His mustache edges fell slightly.

"I mean," I continued, "I think that one's my favorite."

In truth, I knew *The Devil's Dictionary* for one reason, that my dad had a copy and he seemed to have this copy primarily because he liked mentioning that he'd cited one of its entries for his high school yearbook quote: "Cabbage, *n*. A familiar kitchen-garden vegetable about as large and wise as a man's head." I remember thumbing through the book, a collection of similarly irreverent and witty definitions, and allowing it, and the copy of *Bartlett's Familiar Quotations* beside which it was shelved, to shape my early understanding of what a writer did: a writer sat around and came up with little witticisms that would, years later, be misquoted at cocktail parties to a low rumble of approving chuckles and nods. An H.L. Mencken type, or Noel Coward.

In reality, as I began writing myself, I found a better understanding of what writers do in William Styron's *Sophie's Choice*, the beginning of which (I never did finish the book) features the writer-narrator trying to write but repeatedly diverted by the urge to masturbate.

"You know," Ambrose said, continuing to walk, "I was once invited to the White House by none other than Mr. Theodore Roosevelt, and prior to my arrival I made a point of doing my homework. I read, at least cursorily, a representative smattering of his works theretofore published. *The Naval War of 1812, Parts One and Two*, per course, and *The Winning of The West, Volumes One, Two, and Four—Volume Three* is rubbish—but also the lesser knowns such as his study of Gouverneur Morris and the rather peculiar monograph taxonomizing at great length the deer species. Point being, I did this as a matter of propriety. Peppering into our conversation references to, and questions about, the works of one's host is simply written into the social contract." He sighed. "I do not know who sponsored your membership to the Grove, but they surely assumed that you would abide by these courtesies. Perhaps in death you've lost some of these social graces."

"Sponsored? I mean, you invited me. Just now. I've never been here before in my life. Wait, did you say 'in death'? I'm not dead! Right?"

He stopped again, looked at me. "You're not a member?"

"A member? No. I'm not even a member of Costco. I use my brother's card."

"You weren't just taking an evening constitutional as a break from the ceremonies, as I was?"

"Like I said, I've never been here in my life."

"Oh, dear." His fingers combed his mustache. Another sigh. "Well, shit, Kevin."

"Should I leave?"

"Not that simple, is it?" To himself, he mumbled, "Everything is fucked." Then, after another sigh, he said to me, "Fine. I'll be your Virgil. We'll figure out the rest later."

With what felt like the thin membrane encompassing my very ontology quivering, a spiritual nausea, I followed him down the path.

I asked, "What was Teddy Roosevelt like?"

"The man reeked of garlic."

The forest opened up into a massive clearing, at the far end of which was a giant wooden creature—an owl, perhaps, judging from horned ears and lapel-like feathers pulled across its chest—fizzling with flames. In the light of this effigy, dozens of men scattered, more. Others were holding up their drinks, saluting the burning owl sculpture with cheers. Another group of men, clustered like a street-corner doo-wop group, were the ones doing the wolf-howling. A very naked and fantastically fat man wearing a horse-head ran by, chasing someone unseen. Others roamed around in druidic hoods, a few holding torches.

"Quite the sausage party, Ambrose."

"Membership is male only."

"You never heard of the Bechdel Test?" I asked.

"Warren A. Bechtel? Of the Bechtel Corporation? I knew him well. Met him over in Butte when he was working on the Western Pacific. Good man. You won't find him here. A real shame what they did to his work on the Boulder Dam. Hoover shouldn't have his name within twenty leagues of that feat of engineering. Hoover, now there's a fellow you might run into round here. Usually at the craps table."

"I understood nothing of what you just said."

The naked horse-headed man threw a red plastic cup toward the owl effigy, beer spilling out like a comet tail.

"Where can I get one of those?" I asked. "A beer. I mean, I promised myself I wouldn't drink this week, but it seems like that'd be the thing to do, right? I mean, what you said, about a matter of propriety. I think so."

"I'm not sure you intended to say all of that aloud, but there should be a self-serve keg just beyond Priapus there."

He pointed to a towering ice sculpture of a Greek god with a phallus so big he had to hold it up with both arms, like one of those log-tossing brutes at a ren faire. A few men were going at his kneecaps with ice picks, scooping the ice-shards into their cocktails.

"You want me to get you one?" I asked.

"I'm going to get myself a shrub. I'll meet you back here. Don't wander too far."

I went behind Priapus and found the keg at the base of a tree. Hanging from the low branches of the tree were a few plastic bags of wine. A man in a toga walked by, suckled some wine from a bag's spout, then gave it a slap and went on his way.

I grabbed a red plastic cup from the sleeve of them beside the keg and began filling it. The beer was already heady and over-pumped. I sat on the ground beside the keg, crossed my legs, and drank, feeling the foam settle on my upper lip. I must have been pretty thirsty because I quickly drained the beer, and reached for the tap again. I could feel the beer cool me and my encroaching anxiety.

Having a ghost accidentally invite you to a secret

party somehow didn't seem as strange as that same ghost's ominous asides about my own status in the life-death index. Ambrose did seem to have a pretty lucid memory of his own demise, so you'd think that if I'd somehow crossed the Styx, I'd at least be aware of it. I recalled being concerned that a paranoid pot-farmer would atlatl a spear at me if I accidentally stumbled onto his claim, so I checked my body for injury, no signs of my homicide. All was normal. I drank some more beer.

A man approached. I assumed it was Ambrose and said, "Do you mind if I ask you: what am I exactly?" Meaning, was I dead or alive? But since I did not clarify what type of identity-status I was inquiring about, the approaching man was free to interpret as he wished and said:

"You are … an injun."

By now, I could make out his face in the flickering light and saw no benevolent mustache. He had a square face and gray hair pomaded in the style of the old Clark Kent. He was holding a stick horse between his legs.

He said, "I'll be the cowboy."

There was something about his voice—its papery timbre, the way it swooped up at the end of an utterance like a slow, gentle shoveling of words—that I knew somehow.

"You want me to play—"

"Cowboys and Indians," the man said.

"I'm not comfortable—"

"I used to play with Ollie North. He did the best Indian whooping ever. But he's still on the living side, and no one here ever wants to whoop for me."

"Oh God. Oh God. Are you—wait. Could you say something for me?"

"Like a line reading?"

"Yes, could you do a line reading for me?"

"I like doing line readings."

"Could you say, 'Mr. Gorbachev, tear down this wall'?"

"Certainly." He straightened his posture, cleared his throat, and said, "Mr. Globacheck, tear—" He stopped. "Line?"

"That's okay, never mind. I got all I need. It was great." I stood up, walked a few steps closer. I saw the headshot-ready smile, which spread across his face in response to the tiniest bit of praise I'd offered. I saw the slight scrunch of his brow, the folksy sway of his head.

"I could do it another way if you like," Reagan said. "Maybe with an accent?"

"No, no, it was perfect."

"I never get to do accents."

I remembered the day Ronald Reagan had died. I'd been living in L.A. at the time and was stuck in traffic on Santa Monica Boulevard. I turned the radio to NPR and they were playing a collage of different Reagan clips and quotes. The traffic and the news didn't seem related until a police motorcade made its slow way through, escorting a hearse. For the next two weeks, he was interred at a little funeral home in Santa Monica. At the time, I was writing part-time for a local newspaper, while making extra money driving the elderly editor around to do errands five days a week. She made me drive her by the funeral home on every outing. I'd idle on the corner while she told me about Iran-Contra, his support for South African apartheid, and the painfully ham-fisted castration symbolism in his film *Kings Row*. A decade before that, when I'd asked my parents why the trial of the cops who beat Rodney King half to death had been moved to Simi Valley, they told me that's where the Reaganites are and they hate black people.

And now that man—or at least his spectral avatar— was saying to me, "Okay, I played your game, now you play mine. Whoop!"

"Whoop?"

"Not like that. Like an Injun. Give me a good war whoop, and then I'll chase you on my horse. Oh, we can make you a bow and arrow from some branches." It looked for a moment like he was going to head off to find some branches and maybe forget about the thing for now, but then he reshuffled his priorities. "Wait. Take your shirt off."

"What? No."

"Don't you know anything? A real Injun doesn't wear a shirt. Now take it off and whoop."

It felt like his demand had jacklighted me, the way hunters shine flashlights at deer in the middle of the night to stun them still for an easy shot. For a moment, I couldn't move or respond.

He grabbed my T-shirt and tried to pull it up over my head. I resisted and turned and tried to get away, but he was now on top of me, pulling and pulling at my shirt. I fell down and Ronald Reagan tumbled on top of me. Ghost or no, he still had the weight of an old man, and the smell of his body reminded me of the iron-rich taste of blood in the back of your throat after a nosebleed.

It was unclear if he was still trying to get my shirt off or if he now wanted to wrestle, but either way I struggled to get out from under him. When I finally did, scrambling on my knees to get to a safe distance, I looked back and saw him catching his breath, grinning from molar to molar. He picked up his stick horse, wrapped his wrist in the reins, and shouted, "Yee-haw!"

He stepped toward me, the stick horse poised. "C'mon! Gimme a 'whoop'!"

"Okay, okay, okay!" I put my hands up, not sure if he was intending to weaponize the stick horse but not wanting to risk it. "I'll play, I'll play. But first, you have to do something for me." I motioned to him that I was going to stand up, nervous that any sudden movement might be met with him trying to brain me with his toy nag. Getting slowly to my feet, I said, "I'm all for having some fun here, don't get me wrong. But I have a date to FaceTime with my wife and son in the morning, first thing before he goes to preschool, so eventually I got to get some sleep, you know?"

"I'm still not hearing any 'whoop-whoops.'"

"I just mean that I'd love to play your game, but on the condition that you can point me to the path that leads back outta here. Deal?"

"Path out of here? I'm afraid I have no recollection of any path out of the Grove."

"There is, though. I mean, Ambrose. He left, went out to take a piss, found me, and we came back."

"Ambrose? Is that the cocktail Meese is always trying to get me to drink, the one that tastes like licorice?"

"Absinthe, no. I mean Ambrose Bierce."

He idly poked at the dirt with his stick horse. "I have no recollection."

"He's a famous writer. 'An Occurrence at Owl Creek Bridge'? Did you not take AP Lit?"

"Oh, the mustachioed fellow! You know, for years, I thought that was Ring Lardner."

"Yeah, that guy, he left the gates. That's how he found me!"

"Yes, well, Mr. Bierce is a founding member. He's granted certain—privileges. For him, it's more or less an open campus. For the rest of us, well—"

"You're saying I'm stuck here?"

"I'm saying you may have all the time in eternity to give me that 'whoop-whoop,' but that doesn't mean we need to needlessly delay."

I drifted backward a few steps, felt the keg cold on the back of my legs. I sat on the edge of it, breathed. Behind Reagan, beyond Priapus, men were still saluting the effigy, while others strolled more casually in togas, arm in arm, like they were imagining themselves in that Raphael fresco, "The School of Athens," that depicted Plato and Socrates and Aristotle and all those other philosopher kings exchanging their big, important ideas. The self-imagined philosopher kings here, though, already had puddles of vomit to step over in their—not sandals, exactly, but—New Balances.

I hadn't been lying to Reagan about FaceTiming with my family in the morning. At preschool, my son was learning about sea mammals and he liked demonstrating the difference between what a whale sounds like and what a dolphin sounds like.

"Now let's get that shirt off," Reagan said. "Oh, maybe you can put it over your head like a real headdress."

I took a deep breath. Surrounded by death though I may have been, the mountain air and redwood pines still felt refreshing in my lungs.

I said to Reagan, "You'll excuse me if I'm not entirely ready to believe you yet, you know, about not being able to leave. I mean, weren't you the guy who once said that trees cause more pollution than cars?"

He chuckled and said, "Well, it's like my friend Spencer Tracy said, 'Just know your lines and don't bump into the furniture.' Now, speaking of lines, I believe you owe me one. That was the deal."

I figured he was right. I owed it to him. "Can I just leave my shirt on, though?"

"Headdress."

I thought of something. "Feathers. I'll get some feathers. To put in my hair."

He beamed at that idea. "Oh, I like that."

"I know where to find some. You stay right here, okay?"

"Deal!"

"Great!" I backed away from Ronald Reagan, the whole time pointing to his feet and saying, "Stay. Right. There."

And as soon as I was far enough away to be obscured in a dark patch of trees, I turned and ran.

# Three.

Stumbling back out into the clearing, I bumped into a huddle of four elderly men who were struggling to open a can of beer. They were all wearing the same druidic cloaks I'd seen when I first entered, though one was complaining that it was chafing. The others were passing the can around, each trying to get a purchase on the tab to crack it open.

I seized the opportunity—and the beer—to feel useful. "I'll help," I said. This was something I could do. I was, after all, a person of still-living status who had opposable digits with fingernails strong enough to brace the pressure of a beer-can tab. I opened the beer, then sucked the tip of my index finger, as it was now bleeding. The tab had apparently split the nail.

As I sucked the blood from my finger—passing the open beer to the aged revelers—I couldn't help but notice that it didn't have the warm menstrual tang that I would have expected. Perhaps it was already settling, from the white water rapid of living veins to the still, malarial pools of the departed.

"We need a thing, a thing," one of them was saying, making a cranking motion against the newly opened beer. "You know. A shotgun."

"Shotgun? Firearms are back in the armory," another liver-spotted scalp said.

"Not here, they're not. Only on the living side."

"No, you jackanape!" said another. "The thing by which we open the other end of the can, so as to shotgun the beer. So called because it's apparently like getting shot in the face with a beer."

"Cheney isn't here yet—he got an extension."

"We need the thing! For the shotgunning of the beers!"

That conflict-resolution workshop—which I'd taken as part of a professional development week at a copywriting job, the style manual for which had the audacity of insisting that quotations and italics were interchangeable, and during which workshop I had the creeping realization that my presence there was not so much to learn how to resolve conflict as to be the conflict-instigator for others to practice de-escalating— taught me that reflective listening was the first step in empathetic manipulation. So I now said, "I'm hearing that you need to shotgun these beers. Is that correct?"

"Yeah, but bitch-ass Hearst over here thinks he's better than us," said one of the old men, flicking another on the ear. "So if we're gonna do this thing, lil' rosebud licker's gonna have to lick off before we get our beer on."

The man who was the object of this aggression cupped his flicked ear, doubled over, then shot up—shouted, "Gonna fuckin' kill a Kerr tonight!"—and punched his aggressor square in the nose.

And suddenly there were two very old and very dead men in druidic cloaks wrestling on the ground. Bits of their desiccated and decomposing flesh flew off like shrapnel. When one piece landed on my nose, I swiped it off, nearly vomitous upon touching its cold rubberiness.

"Get him, Clark!" said one of the two observers beside me. "Fuck Hearst up good and right!"

The other shouted, "Willy, jack that Kerr up like a fuckin' Model-A!"

Watching William Randolph Hearst aggressively wrestle with Clark Kerr, their fracas kicking up the cool dust from the forest floor, along with sundry bits of body, I realized two things: One, that they were enjoying this, that it was simply part of their usual routine; and two, that hell was other people having fun.

I looked at my split fingernail, now purple with the blood staunched beneath.

Hearst had Kerr in a headlock. The latter tapped out, and they both collapsed into a pile, laughing and wheezing.

I walked away. I wandered by another small huddle of men. Between their shoulders I could see what they were all watching: two people in full-body bear costumes making doggy love on the ground. The plushness of the costumes meant I could not confirm if this involved penetration or merely simulation, but the little gathering watched with the solemn air of expert judges.

I told myself I shouldn't just accept Reagan's version of the rules of this place. He was an idiot. I needed to find Ambrose; he could confirm a few things before I gave myself completely over to despair.

He said he'd gone for a shrub, so I began hunting around the base of the trees where shrubs sprouted pube-like. That led me to a cluster of redwoods by which I found a man in an Ambrose-like suit, on his hands and knees, gathering weeds—the gathering hand furiously swiping the weeds into the holding hand, which had a formidable bouquet of weedlings.

"Pardon," I said.

To which the man said nil.

Again I said, "Pardon."

The man cranked his head to me, clearly startled. He was not Ambrose but had a similar mustache and was wearing a neckerchief that Ambrose surely would have admired. Like a startled animal, he might have been dangerous, so I held up my hands to show I bore no weapons or ill will. I said, "Shrubs?"

He looked at his fistful of plant matter, seemed to relax a bit. "Thyme."

I shrugged. "I dunno. After midnight. I mean, I'm no expert on your whole patrician valhalla here, but does time really exist in a place like this?"

He waved his weeds at the forest. "It's all over. Rosemary and mint, too."

"Got it. Listen, I need Ambrose. He said he was off to get a shrub. You seen a guy rooting around for shrubs? Someone other than yourself?"

He got to his feet, with his free hand brushed the dirt from his pants. "They got shrub at the bar over by the Odin fountain, just beyond Goldwater's treehouse." He looked me over, squinted at my T-shirt. "Ice?"

I looked down at my shirt, tented it out as if to help him read it more clearly, though he'd read it perfectly well. "Ice, ice. And then the arrow to the belly. Get it?"

"Are you batty?"

"No, sorry, I wasn't clear. It was my wife's shirt, from when she was pregnant. Get it? Ice, ice, baby. The baby part you're supposed to infer, you know? Like the song. Okay, shit, so, I know explaining jokes is never funny, but in like, I dunno, 1989 there was this song called 'Ice, Ice, Baby,' okay? And like no one admits to liking it, so that's kinda part of why it's funny when—"

"1989?" he said. "You're new here, then."

"See, it was my wife's when she was pregnant. We put pictures on Instagram and everyone liked it. It's a thing you do. But then after the baby, she lost the baby weight and I started getting fat, so as a joke I started wearing this shirt to bed, but then it just became a habit, and so, basically, I'm still in my pajamas. I didn't know I would be coming here—"

"No one ever does. Some imbecile in a bedsheet invited me here for a drink and then said I couldn't leave. They've been forcing me to do the landscaping ever since. They send me on errands. The thyme is for Coughlin's steak, the nightly offering. If I refuse, that naked fellow in the horse-head hits me. He hits me! I hybridized the apricot and the plum, and now I'm getting cuffed by an inverted centaur."

My heart dipped into my gut. This was Luther Burbank. The Wizard of Horticulture himself was getting back on his knees to pick herbaceous weeds for his abductors' meals. "You said the shrub by the Odin fountain?"

He continued: "And I mean, really, the body of

a human and the head of the horse? I don't mean to inflate my own dirigible but I know something about hybridization, and there's a reason that every mythos on the globe has at least one specter of human and horse mongrelarity, and to a man—or to a whatever—they are all the nag body with the man head. The first aim of crossbreeding is to get the best parts of both subspecies."

"Burbank!" The cranky voice came from the shadows like a bark. "Plant man!"

Luther hunched at the sound, as if anticipating a blow to the back of the head.

A figure came forward, hunched and stiff like a community theater performance of Frankenstein's monster.

"Burbank," the man said, "what is this tomato concoction you delivered for my meatloaf? I asked for ketchup."

Luther cowered beside the base of a tree, holding up his thyme as if to shield himself. "We spoke about this, Mr. Nixon. Tomato is the red in ketchup. Like grapes are the red in wine. Like ultisol soil is the red in clay. I was only—"

"I'm not asking for a horticulture lesson, poindexter. I'm looking for the ketchup that Pat used to pour over my meatloaf! And if you mention Senator Clay again—"

Richard Nixon emerged into the torchlight.

"— I'll make sure you're the next effigy." Nixon crossed his arms and tilted down toward Luther, a gesture so unnatural-looking that it made me wonder if his torso might snap like uncooked spaghetti. "You've been peeping my enemies list, little gardener."

"I haven't, sir, I swear."

"You get me my fucking ketchup now, ninny."

Nixon plucked a twiggy branch from the tree and poked it at Luther. I noticed that his other hand was occupied with a tumbler of brown liquor. Luther got to his feet and, avoiding my eyes, shuffled off.

Somewhere, someone started sing-chanting, "Boola, boola! Boola, boola!" With each round, a few more voices joined in.

Nixon looked at me, said, "The iceman has cometh, I see?"

"Oh. It's my wife's shirt. See, there was this song—actually, you were still alive when it came out. You remember Vanilla Ice?"

"Did you hear what I said?" He pointed his stick at me, continued to growl: "It was a play on words. Did you get it? They never gave Nixon credit as a wit, but I'm clever as hell, goddamnit!" He threw the stick to the ground, took a sip from his drink. "But more to the point, do you have ice?"

"I do not. The shirt's just—you see, on Instagram when you announce that you're pregnant—"

"Don't make me pick that stick back up!" He took another sip of what I could now smell was scotch, peaty enough to singe my nose hairs. "You're new."

"I'm looking for the fountain of Odin."

"Odin, my ass. That thing looks like a fucking golem pissing itself." He drained his scotch. "But I could use a refill. I'll take you."

"That'd be great. Thank you, Mr. Nixon. I'm looking for someone, someone who can get me outta here."

Nixon was looking at his empty glass, slowly rotating it in the firelight, looking at the little rivulets of remaining liquor vine across the glass. "Are you a praying man? Mr.—" He looked at me, his eyebrows gesturing the rest of the question.

"Allardice," I said.

"Huh," Nixon said. "That's a dumb name."

The song—"boola, boola"—was dissolving into a din. I said, "I'm just looking for Ambrose."

"I said: Are you a praying man, Mr. Altaras?" He was shouting now, his body clenched still. "Because I am a praying man, sir. I am. Some say it's foolish to pray in death, but you and I are going to pray. Kneel with me. Come," he said, holding out a hand, "help your president kneel."

"'In death?' I'm not really dead, that's the whole thing."

"Goddamnit, help Nixon kneel."

I stepped forward, took his hand, ice-cold and paper-dry. He clenched, and his fingernails gouged into my skin. He leaned his weight into me and kneeled down in the dirt. He then yanked my arm, indicating that I was to follow. Terrified, I kneeled down beside him. We were facing the base of a redwood as thick around as a mid-size sedan.

Nixon kept his grip on my hand. He said, "Now you can imagine whichever five-armed elephant you like, sir, but when you pray with me it's to my God, got it?"

I could smell moth balls from his cardboard-stiff suit.

He closed his eyes and said, "Dear Lord. Dick here. Been a long time. But you know me, no introductions necessary. Opened China. Made peace with Russia. I'm calling now because if you know one thing about me it's that I'm no quitter. But sometimes, you just have to humble yourself to something greater. It can be overwhelming to look into the sky and know the stars you see have been burnt out for years."

I looked up. I considered this nugget of sophomore dorm-room wisdom (from the same man who once claimed, between slurs against Italians, that he'd make a good Pope). The specter of death and the hope of legacy that was the very sky I took for granted every night was now pulling at me with a greater force. The fortieth president of the United States had recently told me that I was doomed to stay at this death-and-dick party for eternity, and the reality of my irreality I could now feel in my solar plexus, tightening like a screw. I just wanted to FaceTime with my family tomorrow.

"But it seems, dear Lord," Nixon was saying, "that I have an opportunity here, in the guise of this young man. He says he's getting out of here. He says he knows someone who might know the way out. I think it'd be mighty prudent for him to show his president some kindness and let good ol' Nixon tag along. I've been at this goddamn debauch here for too goddamn long, and this young man would be very wise in assisting my liberation."

I knew what he was doing. This was the insidious tactic of parents who no longer communicate—not praying, but speaking to each other through the third-party of a child, rendering him a hollow conduit.

Nixon's God was the hollow conduit through which he was asking for, or demanding, help.

"Mr. Nixon," I said, "I'll do what I can. But I just need to find Ambrose. He brought me here. He has to know how I can get out."

Nixon opened his eyes, looked at me. "You don't know the Master of Revels, then?"

"I only know Ambrose. I think he can get me out."

"Maybe he knows the Master of Revels." He squeezed my hand.

"The what?"

"Only the Master of Revels can approve a release. Your friend must have an in with him."

"Who's the Master of Revels?"

He grabbed my shoulders. His halitosis was like a chemical fog, a chernobyl burp.

He said, "No one admits to knowing. But you find me your friend and we can find out. And if he doesn't give up the name, I know a guy who knows a thing about getting information out of people."

He grabbed my hand, yanked it, and pulled me toward the singing, the "boola, boola," the sound of which seemed to be reconstituting itself from the din. It was a song that would assert itself, only to slip back into chaos, then reammerge, voices finding each other, only to lose each other again, an audible ping-pong game of entropy versus extropy. Cycling back to order was oddly reassuring for my plight.

We emerged into a clearing, a new one. No sight of the owl effigy, no slowly melting Priapus. But: a man flying up into the air. Flailing arms silhouetted between the inky lines of trees. Below him, a group of a dozen men were holding a large bed sheet like a trampoline.

As Nixon and I approached, stepping into the torch-light, I realized that most, if not all, of these men were in states of partial or complete undress.

I asked my companion, "What's with all the dick flapping around here?"

"That's not my penis," Richard Nixon said, "that's my nose. And I'll thank you not to stare."

# Four.

"You know," Richard Nixon said, "if you can help out ol' Dick here, and we can find ourselves on the other side of those gates, I might be able to get you something in return. How'd you like an ambassadorship? You'll have to help me on which countries still exist, but we can work it out."

I felt both the urgent need to ditch Nixon and a vague sense that he could actually help me somehow, that whatever leverage he had could be of use. I wasn't sure what an ambassador did, but—in the moments before the idea of a dead man implying political influence over a still-living realm made my binary sense of living and dead collapse, giving me a spell of vertigo—I plumed at the idea. Ambassador Allardice. Maybe a sash would be involved. Silk, with a seal and tassels.

Then the dead man said, "I've always been an optimist, you know? Been stuck here for twenty years, more—time exists here, which is the worst part, they really make you feel each second—but I've known things would one day work out. That's something everyone gets wrong about me. I try to live on the sunrise side of the mountain. If you just trust that things will work out, they will. It's when you turn pessimist, nihilist, that's when things go wrong."

I guess all those civilians in Cambodia, then, just didn't have enough faith in the benevolence of the universe. I was about to quip something to this effect, but I still cowered in the face of authority, even when that face was one that had been decomposing *en plein air* since the 1990s (gray and purple tabs of flesh flecking off in the breeze, a viscous material pooling around his nostrils and behind his ears). Any iconoclasm or even irreverence I harbored lived solely in my internal monologue, showing only through the fissures in my outward obsequiousness. Once, when a boss of mine mumbled, re: the color of a memo cover page, that he liked mauve, I simultaneously said-shouted that I loved mauve while internally raging at anyone who'd say mauve instead of purple, and somewhere in my brain some potential neural pathway that could have led to great ideas, epiphanies, inventions, forever closed.

We approached a large picnic table, big as a full-size American flag. Perhaps that comparison jumped to mind because the entire surface of the table was covered in a gigantic Pyrex dish in which someone had designed a fruit flag: strawberries arranged in lateral rows alternating with slices of banana, the upper left-hand corner a block of blueberries with blueberry-less gaps for stars. I plucked a strawberry and ate it, felt the perfumey ping of gin on my tongue. I ate a few more, until my brain felt as booze-soaked as the fruit.

Nixon said, "H.W. brought this. New guy. Thinks he's still at some sort of Kennebunkport potluck."

"Seems to be missing some stars," I said.

"H.W. never approved of the Dakotas."

I plucked a couple berries from the block of blue in the corner, made room for the Dakotas.

A man rushed up, a man whose white mutton chops fluttered at his cheeks like the ambassador sash I'd never get to wear, and grabbed Nixon by his shoulders. Nixon's suit jacket collapsed in enough for me to see just how much his musculuature had decomposed beneath it. Like an anorexic in a David Byrne suit. This new man—who was short, stout, and so old I wasn't sure if his billowy poncho was a toga-like costume or simply a remnant of his time—pulled Nixon down to his level and said, "We're doing the Harvard-Yale game of '33 tonight, and we need a Handsome Dan."

"Not again, Philbert." Nixon tried to twist away, but the gargoyle pulled him closer. I could see the embers from the sizzling effigy in the haze of his exhalations. "We're doing the whole game. We need someone to play the Yalie bulldog, and you're the favorite for the role. We're gonna do the dog-napping, the whole deal. You'll have to wear the leash, so come on!"

Nixon looked at me with what seemed like sad bulldog eyes, and said, "I don't like the leash. It chafes. Help me, Mr. Altaras."

"My name is Allardice."

Nixon tried to grab my hand, but Philbert had him tight by the shoulders; this meant that Nixon could only move his lower arms so he flailed at me like a T-rex. The mustache man pulled Nixon away, off into the dark din of shouts: "Handsome Dan! Handsome Dan!"

I was free. For once, my passivity had served an active role: my inaction had freed me from Richard Nixon. Like pretending to forget a jury summons. Only if that jury summons were the decaying corpse of an American president.

Anxious to flee the scene before Nixon came back, I turned, ran, and before I could make it two strides, a football concussed me in the face.

I blinked awake on the ground. In the moment before the players descended upon me, I enjoyed the dark vista above, the stars like diamonds scattered across black velvet. But then, they came, the two phalanxes of seal-like bodies, colliding against each other. When the bodies crashed down on me, it felt less like I was being smothered by living creatures than by burlap laundry bags stuffed with damp towels gone to mildew. I twisted beneath the weight, fought to find a pocket of air. I was able to prop myself up on my elbows just enough to breathe without the weight above preventing my lungs from expanding. The pile of bodies above—and what felt like a chaos of elbows—soon untangled themselves and dispersed, and I pushed myself to my feet.

Here's what I saw: a scramble of elderly men, in sundry stages of decay, running, with surprising alacrity, toward a football rolling around, having surely just landed, at the far end of the clearing. Half the men were clothed in an assortment of Greek and Roman cosplay, seersucker suits, and male sartoria so dated that shirts looked like '80s-era power blouses. The other half of the players were shirtless, glistening in the moonlight. From my brow, I wiped some sweat that I realized might not have been my own, and I hastily flapped my hand dry in the breeze.

Shirts versus skins, the game seemed to be. Harvard versus Yale, if I'd heard correctly from the man who absconded with Nixon.

Nixon: who was now on the sidelines wearing a collar around his neck as dainty as a lace choker, clipped to a leash held by the man who was simultaneously painting a Y on the front of Nixon's chest. The man doing the leash-holding and the painting was fully clothed, so if he was a representative of the Harvard side, having dog-napped Nixon's Handsome Dan bulldog, that meant that Harvard was shirts and Yale skins.

I paused, standing there in the middle of their ad hoc football field, to wonder why I'd taken the time and brainspace to puzzle through which team was which.

And that's when I saw him: Ambrose Bierce. On the sidelines, just over Nixon's hunched shoulders. A bit blurry in the dark, but I recognized his mustache, the rigid flection of his posture. I had to get to him, but I didn't want to alert Nixon that I'd found my man—couldn't just go up the middle, then, had to take an end-around, dropping back and down the line of play.

Once I was safely obscured by the players, who were now slapping at each other, the ball rolling around at their feet (if this was a reenactment of some famous game, I'm pretty sure it didn't go down in the history books for open-palm cheek-swatting), I made a dash for the end-zone—assuming the scarves tied to dirt-stuck sticks marked the boundaries of the end-zone. I thought I could sneak from there into the surrounding trees and circle around to Ambrose. But when I was just a meter from the end-zone, I was tackled by a shirtless man, my body going ragdoll against his velocity. The man, sweating a cold, chilling sweat, had surely mistaken me—wearing a shirt, after all—for a Harvard man.

As this luminary of public life picked himself off me, I felt either the sharp pang of a rib breaking or the sharp pride of being mistaken for a Harvard man. I picked myself up, and my tackler ran to the huddle of skins, liver spotted and patched with hair, the whole group heaving together with collective breath.

I tried to get a visual on Ambrose, but behind Nixon I now just saw darkness, trees, and flickers of candlelight. I abandoned my original play and made a run for where he'd been standing. Nixon seemed too dispirited to notice me. About a stride from the sidelines, I was again—by a shirtless ghoul—tackled.

This tackler was frailer, his frame more Coolidge than Taft—maybe it actually was Coolidge—so I recovered relatively quickly, but I was still fuming by the time I got back to my feet and shouted at the player, "I'm not in the game! For fuck's sake, I'm not in the fucking game!"

Behind me, Nixon said, "Of course you're in the game. There's no escaping it."

I quickly moved to the sidelines. The man holding

Nixon's leash was incanting quietly, "Fight fiercely, Harvard! Fight, fight, fight!"

Nixon slowly turned to me and said, "You let them take me. You abandoned your president. You're going on the list."

His captor snapped the leash. "Quiet, dog!" He then continued his song—"Hurl that spheroid down the field and fight! Fight! Fight!"—a single tear beading in his cornea.

Beyond them, I saw a figure in the darkness. Not that of Ambrose; this figure was beyond any human scale, and there appeared to be horns sprouting from the giant's head.

I walked around Nixon and the Harvard man, and I headed for Odin's fountain.

Odin—carved, it seemed, from a redwood—stood a good ten feet tall, and he struck a victor's stance, one leg resting on the severed head of a giant wolf. One hand was extended, palm up, holding a hawk; the other gripped a spear, at ease. His chest was carved with care, muscles so pronounced it looked like he was smuggling potatoes beneath his skin, wormed with veins. Equally vascular was his dick, sticking straight out as if pointing to some hopeful future. From the tip sprayed—with a firehose force—a continual stream of what I could smell was red wine. Men stumbled by, drank from the stream, and continued on their way.

I looked around for shrubs, saw the usual fluff of minor greenery. I recalled all the weeding I'd failed to do in life, the way I'd casually let our garden get choked by volunteers, as I'd learned to call weeds.

I was already thinking about life in the past tense.

Suddenly beside me was a man in a tuxedo, holding a tray on which stood a single martini glass—the shape echoing the shape of his splayed fingers beneath the tray—and he said, in a voice like the hum of a ceiling fan, "Can I get you anything?"

"Shrub," I said.

"Certainly."

"Or rather, I'm looking for a man who said he wanted shrubs."

But the waiter was already gone, leaving behind only a vague whiff of bathroom potpourri, something dry, mossy, and lavender-like that had absorbed years of fecal dust.

I walked toward the nearest patch of weeds, on the lookout for any dark shape in the forest that could be Ambrose, when suddenly the waiter was at my side again, one claw-like hand on my shoulder.

He said, "Sir."

"Jesus Christ!"

He smirked. "Close."

"You scared the shit out of me."

"Your shrub." He no longer had the tray, but handed me a pink cocktail in a tall, skinny Tom Collins glass.

I took the glass. "A shrub is a drink?"

"And a popular one." He took his hand off my shoulder, looked at his fingers and rubbed them, as if to clean off some ectoplasm my body had dirtied him with. I looked at my shoulder, didn't see anything. The waiter wiped his hand on the towel hanging over his other forearm, then he continued: "Yours is the second shrub I've served tonight."

I took a sip, and as soon as the cool liquid hit my lips I realized how dehydrated I was, began gulping the pink stuff down. The piss-like acidity of vinegar aerated my sinuses, and I choked a bit. My instinct was to do a hacky spit-take, but it came out more pukey than comical, and the waiter backed away from me like I was fit for quarantine.

Something occurred to me. "Wait!" I wiped my chin. "Wait—who'd you serve the other to?"

The waiter paused, said, "I don't believe he finished drinking it. I noticed him in the stocks. He's a favorite target of Buckley, you know."

I must have registered confusion on my face, because the waiter added a clarifying nod over his shoulder. Over there, at the base of a tree, was a man slumped on the ground, his feet locked in wooden stocks.

I ran over, placed my hand on his back, and Ambrose looked up, his eyes shaded with exhaustion. He wheezed, "Buckley."

"It's me," I said.

He exhaled, the staticky sound of emphysema. He said, "Is that—" pointing to the glass still in my other hand.

I took the cue and tilted the glass to his mouth. He drank the whole thing, in big gasping gulps, even crunching the ice between the gray nubs of his teeth.

I had a brief flare of parental pride, nourishing this sad soul. Maybe this wasn't mother's milk, but a pissy cocktail would do. It did, after all, seem to revive the man to a state of alertness again. When my wife was breastfeeding, I'd linger in the doorway, desperately wishing my own body could provide such vital nourishment, while neglecting to move that same dumb body into action to load the dishwasher.

"Oh, that's the stuff," Ambrose said.

I checked the stocks, locked with a padlock the size

of a soup bowl, calcified and rusted to a gritty scrape on the hand.

His eyes widened, focused on something just above me.

"Buckley," he whispered.

"I think people here keep mishearing my name," I said.

Behind me, a voice: "My guest tonight is a man who should need no introduction, and so perhaps the introduction I will now give suggests the timidity of that so-called legacy."

This voice was squeezed to an ineffectual timbre by a transatlantic vagueness of vowels. A breeze on my neck might as well have been the breath of this groaning man.

I turned, saw a man unfolding a folding chair, then folding himself into it. He was well suited, more modernly so than the rest, and he progressed to lean so far sideways in his chair I thought he'd just topple over onto the pine needles. But he didn't. This man somehow maintained an angle of lean that certainly marked him as beyond the canny, this man whose ophidian non-smile and saliva'd combover also marked him as someone I suddenly knew: William F. Buckley, Jr.

As a kid, if Bob Ross's *The Joy of Painting* on PBS didn't put me cozily to sleep, I was then stuck with the reruns of William F. Buckley, Jr.'s *The Firing Line*, a show that presented an often—because of the network's syndication algorithm—ahistorical topicality, arguments about the '79 gas crisis airing again in the mid-90s, in voices that initially seemed tonally harmonious with that of Mr. Ross, but whose undercurrent of hatred would only become legible in the nightmares that would follow.

The ghost of William F. Buckley, Jr. said, while tonguing the stem of a pipe, "Mr. Ambrose Bierce, once thought the wit of his age, is now largely forgotten."

I realized Buckley—whose voice was like an unformed but unhurried bowel movement, slinking out with a clay-like tactility—seemed to be mugging to an imagined audience, or what I hoped was an imagined audience. Maybe there was a camera and live studio audience hidden in the dark forest behind me.

The host continued: "I've invited my guest on the program tonight because I hear so many around this grove of ours encomiating and panegyrizing the cleverness of Mr. Bierce, and yet he has continually denied my invitations to appear on the program. But hesitancy is nothing the ol' stocks can't remedy, I've found."

I heard a chuckle, crepitated by the sporadic light clap, and I realized that there was, in fact, an audience behind me, one apparitioned by the very suggestion that they were there. About two dozen people were suddenly gathered in seats, beneath what felt like studio lights, flood lights, glaring down upon us.

Buckley, holding a stack of notecards in one hand, angled his head to peruse them through the lower half of his bifocals, and said, "Mr. Bierce, my first question—" He stopped, spotting me obscuring his view of his guest.

"Oh, hello, we appear to have a third member of our panel tonight." He pursed his lips, an anus-like pucker. "Tell me, how may I and our increasingly less patient studio audience be of help to you?"

The studio he spoke of was still the redwood forest, but with just enough markers of a television studio— the lights, mostly, and the sudden audience—for me to question if I were still here. Sure enough, my feet shuffled some pine needles. I said, "I suppose—I need to know who the Master of Revels is."

The audience laughed in that canned way, and Buckley chuckled.

"Well," he said, "it's charming that you took my passive aggression as genuine. I guess in my dotage and death, my rapier has been dulled a bit. But I find your nescience intriguing. And if television has taught me anything it's that a good debate is predicated on proper incentivization. So, how about this? I have prepared here some questions for my scheduled guest, that man there looking Kent-like in the stocks." He flicked a finger at Ambrose. "Why don't I pose them to the two of you—the most satisfactory respondent will be granted his goal. Best two out of three. You said you'd like to know the identity of the Master of Revels, and Mr. Bierce, what shall we say would be your prize?"

Ambrose raised his head. "Freedom would be nice."

Buckley said, "Well, there you go. The stakes are set. First question."

## FIVE.

"Wait," I said. "What counts as a good answer? I mean, what's the rubric?"

Buckley puckered his lips as if for a kiss, a gesture of genuine contemplation, it seemed. He said, "Well, our studio audience is the best judge. This is, after all, a democracy."

The crowd gave a good laugh, as if testing for audio levels. Buckley nodded his approval at them.

"You know, dear boy, you're rather antsy," Buckley said to me. "And that just won't do. You see, in the television business, you need to, as they say, find your light. That is, hit your mark and stay on it. Sometimes assistance is needed." Buckley waved his index card, and from the darkness hurried two men dressed like medieval tanners, or modern-day leather fetishists. They were holding a large piece of lumber featuring two holes in the middle.

I was so stunned to see that they were putting me in stocks that by the time I did realize it, they'd already done it.

The larger of the henchmen had been surprisingly accommodating as he eased my ankles into the stocks, like a nurse helping you onto a gurney, and they were both now shuffling off back into the shadows.

Ambrose and I sat there on the ground, both pairs of feet locked in wood.

The stocks were fresh-cut, the foot-holes splintery on my ankles.

"All right, now, let's see." Buckley, leaning sideways in his chair, his combover the only thing offering a counterweight, riffled through his index cards. "When the Sphinx asked Oedipus what creature walks on four legs in the morning, two legs at noon, and three in the evening, Oedipus's correct answer of 'man' caused the death of the Sphinx. Most focus on the fate of Oeddy, but as the interviewer I must focus on the fate of the asker. After all, I'm already dead. I have no interest in a second death." He mugged to the audience, whom I couldn't see clearly behind the glare of the light. "We all know where that leads." The audience's laughter sounded frayed as if by analogue tape decay. "But riddles it shall be," and he began an epic throat-clearing session.

I tried to clear my head, concentrate. I had just enough familiarity with the history of riddles in literature, specifically the use of riddles as a test of character, to be nervous. I wasn't much for puzzles. I had once bought one of those brain-buster books at Barnes and Noble, from the impulse-buy rack beside the register, thoroughly believing the jacket copy that its curation of cryptograms, logic puzzles, and philosophical thought-experiments would transform the breeze-shaken daffodil of my brain into a clear, cutting thorn. In my haste to be some sort of Sherlockian figure-outer of the world, as if the world were built on anything resembling logic, I misread the quote on the front of the book ("Logic is the Keystone to Reality"—Stephen Pinker) as a blurb of endorsement rather than a simple citation. At home—or rather, in my car at a stop light—I spent an hour or a minute flipping through the book, hating myself for not being good at thinking.

It was, perhaps, a vestigial anxiety from my college days, when I'd taken a literature course from a professor who was actually a philosophy professor but seemed to be in the midst of jumping from one sinking departmental ship to another, who taught the great Rubik's Cubes of literature—the Pynchonian branch of the family tree—and all the coursework seemed to circle around decoding riddles, all of which I failed miserably. When from Joyce's *Ulysses* the professor read, "The cock crew, the sky was blue: The bells in heaven were striking eleven. 'Tis time for this poor soul to go to heaven,"

I raised my hand and said, "I'm noticing some phallic imagery in here," and the professor responded, "There are such things as real answers, you know." When he later posed Samson's riddle from The Book of Judges—"Out of the eater, something to eat; out of the strong, something sweet"—I tried to redeem myself by saying, "He seems to be using chiasmus," and a moment later my professor threw a dry-erase marker at my head.

Point being, I was nervous at the idea of a riddle. Even watching *Labyrinth*, I would get sweaty during the scene in which Jennifer Connelly must choose one of two doors in order to progress in the Labyrinth, and one of the two Muppet-guards on the medieval seal says one door leads to the castle in the center of the Labyrinth, "while the other one leads to Certain Death!" When Jennifer Connolly tries to engage with the riddlers, they say, "One of us always tells the truth, and one of us always lies." Even as an adult, I knew my wits were no match for fourteen-year-old Jennifer Connolly, and even after watching the film countless times, I could never remember, much less figure out, the riddle.

Not to mention all those brain teasers that Tom Hanks's dimly mulletted academic riddled through in those Da Vinci movies—pretzels of logic that seemed not only beyond my capacity, but that toggled at the precipice of life and death. That was the precipice I seemed to be teetering on right now.

Buckley's throat was finally clear of phlegm, and he said, "Are you ready?"

I said, "I guess." I figured Buckley was enough of a literary aspirant that I might luck out and get one of the great riddles of the western canon from that college class, if only I remembered the answers.

To my right, Ambrose said, "Mmmph."

"Here we go," Buckley said. He adjusted his stack of index cards, as if shuffling the loose letters into their proper places, as only the true diviner of their wisdom could. "Would you rather be a tree or a fish?"

I waited for the rest of the riddle, figured this was just the pause before the dependent clause that enumerated the world of this hypothetical, filled it with all sorts of existentially barbed realities, both arboreal and ichthyological. But no. That was the end of the question. I looked at Ambrose, but he was slumped in a depression, his slow breath gently disturbing his mustache.

"We'll go with the pimpled one first," Buckley said.

I suppose the question was really a matter of mobility: the freedom to move, but only through water, or a life rooted to the earth. Although being trapped in these wooden stocks had me itchy with claustrophobia, and mosquito bites, there was something about a tree's life that seemed beyond minor anxieties, whereas a fish's life, though mobile, seemed animated by the essence of anxiety: an awareness only of one's status as prey.

"I'd rather be a tree," I said.

Ambrose, without looking up, said, "I'm a fish withering on the shore of the sea of thought."

Buckley said, "Okay, studio audience, by show of applause, who votes fish?"

From beyond the glare of the stage lights came a small smattering of claps.

"And votes for tree?"

Applause clicked on, a raucous ovation, which then ended with an audible click.

"They have spoken," Buckley said. "The fish is the loser."

From some unseen above dropped a large, dead fish. It landed on Ambrose's head—some cold, fishy water splashing on me—then slid down the side of his face to land—eyeless, I saw—on the dirt between us. The studio audience ripped open in grotesque laughter.

"Lovely," Buckley said. His chuckle echoed in the base of my skull like the death rattle.

I itched my mosquito bites.

"Excuse me," I said. "If a mosquito bites me, does that mean that my blood is still living?"

The unseen studio audience gave a murmuring laugh.

Buckley said, "I've been dead for a decade and they're all over me. Okay, next conundrum."

I kept scratching at the cluster of bites on my forearm until blood emerged. I tasted the blood, held it on my tongue like a sommelier searching for the dim tang of life. I tasted nothing.

"Would you rather eat," Buckley continued, "a worm or a spider?"

"Wait, sorry," I said, wiping any evidence of blood from my lip, "is this just a round of Would You Rather? I thought this would be riddles or something? Like crucibles of character."

Buckley said, "Cute tangle of phrase, but it's the simple choices that define our lives and our ability to navigate it. Whereas a riddle can ponder the hypothetical, and thought experiments can ask fascinating questions like, 'Is the cat dead or alive?' those are ultimately questions for the fantasist who refuses to live in the world. I, however, am a pragmatist. My feet are on the ground." He realized at that moment that his feet were in fact propped on a stump that served as an ottoman, and he quickly returned them to the dirt. He took a puff of his pipe. "And so I believe in the value of focusing our energies on the vital questions that face us and our republic every day. Now, would you rather eat a worm or a spider?"

I looked at Ambrose. He had fish viscera on his cheek. He finally looked back at me. He shrugged.

I was confused by the game theory being employed here. If every question was a binary, and there were two players, then the second responder didn't really have a choice, and there seemed to be no system in place here to determine who would respond first. The rubric was beginning to feel almost tesseract-like in its—

Buckley said, "Come on now, answer. We haven't got eternity."

I remembered the impact of that professor's dry-erase marker making contact with my temple.

"Spider," I said.

"Worm," Ambrose said.

"Worm is correct," Buckley said. "The spider is the loser."

"What about the audience deciding?" I asked. "The applause-o-meter?"

Instead of a response I received a handful of spiders

dropped on my head. Once again, the studio audience let loose with vicious laughter.

The spiders were tiny little goblin hands tickling my scalp. I shivered, frantically shook my head. I swatted at them, felt them fall away. One scurried down my shirt. I yanked at it, scratched at it. I couldn't get the spider off, so I just pulled my shirt up and swatted at my bare skin until I saw that last spider shuffle away. I leaned back, took a breath, tried to suppress the particular horror induced by myriad insectoid legs, a number presumably divisible by eight, prickling my body.

"Next and final conundrum. For the tie-breaker, how about a nice one? Would you like a nice one for a change?"

Ambrose and I gravely nodded.

"Would you rather," Buckley said, "be able to play the piano or ride an elephant?"

I swallowed. I looked up, saw nothing but dark potential. If I got this wrong, either an elephant or a piano would descend upon me from above, that yawning abyss occupied, presumably, by the *Loony Tunes* prop department. Maybe there was some game theory being employed here after all. The right answer was not so much about our preference as it was about Buckley's preference—what did he feel like dropping on his contestants, *Double Dare*-like?

I looked at Ambrose. Fear veined his eyes.

An elephant seemed to have the air of the British occupation of India, so maybe that had something to do with it? Maybe Buckley would love to see one of us squashed beneath an elephant. But then: a piano? A symbol of aristocratic refinement, perhaps? Maybe he'd prefer one of us crushed by that.

Or another way to approach it: one, the elephant, would be a blunt impact, whose after-wreckage would involve a live animal writhing atop you; whereas the other, the piano, would provide a perhaps sharper after-wreckage, what with all its wires and sundry machinery. Was this a matter of decoding not the torture's symbolism but its efficacy, and if so the torturer's personal aesthetic of pain, sharp or dull? Yes, I thought. After all, Buckley just said he was a pragmatist, had less interest in empty symbolism. And he valued, I guessed, the sharp laceration of a piano wire over the blunt impact of an elephant falling on you.

Buckley said, "Your answer, Ambrose?"

So much for game theory. I was stuck with whatever choice Ambrose didn't pick. Life has no logic. If you get crushed by a piano or an elephant you still get crushed, and you have no say in the matter.

"Elephant," Ambrose said.

My choice was set. "Piano," I said.

William F. Buckley hitched one wiry eyebrow up a few rungs. "Elephant," he said, "is the loser." And he waved his index cards.

Ambrose grabbed my arm. I grabbed his hand. I yanked him, but with the stocks on our feet, as we attempted to roll away from the elephant's landing zone, we must have resembled a couple of ill-puppeted marionettes flopping around. Regardless of grace, I managed to pull Ambrose a few yards away by the time we heard—or felt—the pachyderm descend. When something that size is falling above you, it's the air that tells you, the way it suctions itself, like the way the water before a wave sucks itself out before crashing in.

By the time the elephant landed, Ambrose and I had rolled—clunkily, woodenly—just far enough away to be safe. The creature hitting the earth sounded like a hundred bagpipes played by a steam engine. And then: the leathery, meat-squish of tree-thick legs flailing for footing. And then: the airhorn of the beast's despair. A fanfare of pain. I could feel the sonic-boom of its landing, pointilated by bits of musky matter I wanted to remain ignorant of.

Point being, though, I'd saved Ambrose from the falling beast. I continued to roll the man, our stocks clunking along, pulling us to what felt like a safe distance, behind a cluster of trees, through which Buckley's studio lights cast an expressionistic chiaroscuro. My ankles hurt like hell.

Once away from the glare of Buckley's show, I found a skull-size stone, which proved adequate in smashing our legs free of the stocks. The trick was to cease the smashing in the moment before it got to the ankles. The splinters were bothersome.

Finally free, Ambrose rubbed his ankles and I scrambled to look around the tree. Buckley and his lights and his audience had disappeared. I saw only the little comma of his pipe there in the dirt.

I sat beside Ambrose, shook the memory of the spiders from my neck. "Buckley has disappeared."

"I am most obliged to your pulling me from the path of that falling creature."

"Yeah," I said. "It's just that I won and now there's no one to give me my prize."

"Which was?"

"The identity of the Master of Revels."

"Oh, heck," Ambrose said, "I can give you that." He pushed himself to his feet. "But my more immediate concern is staying out of the way of that elephant. You can hear him out there—he's on a must."

I stood up. "You know who the Master of Revels is? Who? And can you get me to him? He's the only one who can get me out of here!"

"The Master of Revels," Ambrose said—and my mind raced: which wielder of power was the Great and Powerful Oz of the Bohemian Grove's hellscape?—"is Father Coughlin."

My mind blinkered. "Who?"

# Six.

We quickly saw the damage wrought by the elephant. The splintered remains of Odin were strewn along the ground in a path diagonal across the clearing. There, his head; bits of torso about; limbs scattered as if from an explosion at the old mannequin factory. In the middle of it all, a pool of red wine was sending tentacle streams out in all directions. In the center of the pool, Hearst crouched, cradling Odin's severed cock, the tip still dribbling wine. "Dear one," he said. "Dear one."

From the surrounding forest came the screams of men, by which you could track the path of the elephant. It seemed to be circling around and heading this way. Ambrose grabbed my arm, pulled. As we ran, I glanced behind me and caught only a blurred glimpse of the charging elephant emerging into the clearing, beneath a halo of broken branches.

Ambrose pulled me behind a tree. The elephant stampeded by. While he didn't hit us, a wave of his musk did, thick enough to make my eyes water. I thought we were safe, but Ambrose said, "Climb. He's going in ellipses. He'll come back around. Climb." Then Ambrose began climbing up the trunk of the redwood.

Sure enough, there were wooden slats nailed there in a makeshift ladder. I followed.

It was harder than I anticipated, each rung having only an inch of surface on which to leverage all your weight. But I made it up to the door in the floor of what appeared to be a sizable treehouse. I pulled myself up. Ambrose covered the door with a wood panel.

The treehouse that we found ourselves in was like a large crow's nest, a self-contained balcony with a tree running through the middle. It was enclosed by a nipple-high railing, on which Ambrose was now leaning, looking down. I joined him. Below, in the flickering light of the still-smoldering owl effigy, we could see the odd scramble of men.

"Where's Orwell when you need him?" I said.

"Not here, that's for sure."

We were about twenty feet up, but it was high enough for me to feel my vertigo coming on. I stepped back from the edge, sat down with my back against the tree. "Sorry," I said. "Was just feeling dizzy or something. I'm supposed to keep an eye on my blood pressure. Gotta keep it under one-forty over ninety."

Ambrose walked over to me. "One-forty? No, it's about half-past midnight. But time doesn't matter here."

"No, my blood pressure. It's—never mind. Earlier

this year I had a thing, a—cardiac event. It's a genetic thing. I mean, yes, I've gained some weight, but it's just a hereditary condition. I was supposed to relax up here. See, at first I thought it was just a panic attack but—"

"You've mistaken my countenance for one of curiosity, but I assure you the angle of my brow is not meant to solicit personal revelations. It's just a—as you say—hereditary condition." He lowered his hand for me. "We can't stay here forever."

I took his hand and he pulled me to my feet.

"This is Barry's place, and he gets a mite territorial."

"So who's this guy?"

"Who, Barry? He's the ignoramus who—"

"No, no. Father something. The Master of Revels? Who is he and where can I find him?"

Ambrose inhaled. He fluffed his mustache. "Radio Priest. Rather bellicose. Not a fan of the Jews. Or Protestants. Or Muslims. Or Jews. Or people hailing from the Lower Americas, or from the Upper Africas, or the Lower Africas. Or the suffragettes. Or..."

Ambrose wandered back over to the edge of the treehouse, gazed down at the scattered screams and scamperings, and I couldn't make out the rest of the litany. He propped a booted foot on a crook of the rail, rested his elbow on his knee, his chin on his hand, as if posing for a yearbook photo, and his senior quote just happened to be the Wikipedia entry of a fascist.

"Reached tens of millions of ears through his radio broadcasts. He once used that influence on behalf of the New Deal, but then something changed. Started in with the America First stuff, the Christian Front stuff. He was the first man, it seems, to figure the power of that medium, the immediacy of it, the intimacy of the voice. Began using that loudspeaker, reaching all those ears, to bring people into the fascist cause. Folks said he was persuasive, but mostly he was just loud."

My back against the tree, I said, "And this guy's the only one who can sign my release?"

"He keeps himself in the aviary. Enjoys the company of exotic birds. Be forewarned, though, he has two henchmen—one attacks by mechanisms of air, the other by mechanisms of land."

Ambrose turned to me. His face was in silhouette, flares of hair catching the backlight, the firelight, for a hellish halo.

"I can't help you win that one."

"Win?"

Something moved beneath my feet—I feared the structure was failing, that this was the overture to freefall. Turns out, I was standing on the panel covering the door in the floor, and the panel was suddenly lifting. As I stepped off the panel, it moved away to reveal the elevating head of a man whose white hair was slicked back and spiked with a single arrow from his leather headband, a man whose beady eyes were framed in black rims.

He tossed a bow—carved, it seemed, from a redwood branch and strung with something flossy—onto the floor of the treehouse, then hoisted himself up. He was shirtless, torso like a melted candle, and he had a quiver of arrows slung over his shoulder. Despite the getup, he was wearing slacks and dress shoes. He at first took no notice of me and Ambrose, as he was focused on finding his bow. He looked for it with the stooped leer of the short-sighted. His glasses must have needed a new prescription. He grabbed the bow from the floor, stood up, and finally saw us, or maybe just our blurry forms.

"Intruders!" He reached for an arrow in his quiver. As he did so, his body turned, the quiver shifting just out of his reach. So he kept turning, like a music box ballerina, hand and arrow maintaining equal distance. When he'd made a full turn, the quiver slipped from his shoulder and the arrows clattered to the floor. He got to his knees—a hatchet, hilt feathered and ribboned, falling from his belt—and began gathering the arrows. Once he'd arranged them back into the quiver, he took one out, placed the quiver on the floor, and fit the arrow into the bow. Still on his knees, he aimed it—shakily— at Ambrose.

He cleared his throat—"Intruders"—then turned the arrow to me.

I held up my hands.

Ambrose held out his open palms and said, "Now listen here, Goldwater, this here, uh, affray is not needed for either party. And—might you proffer a brief gloss of your getup? My God, sir, I can see your teats!"

Barry Goldwater looked down. His posture seemed to cave in a moment of body-shame. Then he puffed up again, aimed the arrow true. "I'm an Injun! Hopi!" He cleared his throat. "Whoop, whoop!"

"Oh, you should go play with Reagan," I said and immediately regretted it, as I suddenly had Goldwater's—and his arrow's—attention.

The arrowhead was shaky, its potential energy about to turn kinetic.

"You seen him?" Goldwater said.

I shook my head. "I mean, not recently."

"I was hoping I could ambush him from up here."

He lowered the arrow and, pushing past Ambrose,

shuffled to the edge of the treehouse. He looked down, the little darting movements of his head suggesting he was following the trajectories of multiple men on the ground. His gaze started darting faster and faster, his eyeglasses catching the firelight in little flashbulb flares, and that's when we heard it: the doppler-compressed roar of the elephant tearing another path of destruction down below. Scattered screams in its wake. Ambrose ran to the ledge beside Goldwater, and shouted, "Heinous!"

The hatchet was on the floor, half-a-dozen feet away. Goldwater's back was turned. With my eyes on him, I inched sideways toward the weapon.

Goldwater began to pull the arrow back again, but even without looking over the edge, I could tell the elephant was no longer beneath us. I could feel it stomping away, like a pulse in the earth beating up the tree to my feet. Ambrose put his hand on Goldwater's wrist, said, "Hold."

Surprisingly, Goldwater did.

Ambrose said, "Too bad Barnum isn't here. He could probably tame that thing into performing some diverting little jig."

Goldwater lowered his bow and turned to Ambrose. "Yes, and why isn't he here? Did he never get an invite?

When I arrived I somehow thought I'd be able to meet him. You know"—Goldwater perked up and seemed to be forgetting the whole "Intruder" overture to our relationship—"I saw the most delightful show of his once, years after his passing, of course. It featured a song duet between a great fat man with shoe-polish on his face and a dwarf"—Goldwater was bouncy with chuckles—"and they were singing while on a seesaw, and you can imagine"—but he couldn't finish for his laughter, which had the rusted weeze of smoker's cough.

I bent down and grabbed the hatchet, thinking I could quickly tuck it into the back of my pants' waist. It was heavier than I'd anticipated. The handle was worn smooth from the grip of countless hands. I took a second to graze the edge of the blade with the pad of my thumb, and found it sharp, the delicate scrape of its fine edge finding each furrow of my fingerprint like corduroy.

My moment of distraction was Goldwater's moment of action. He was suddenly on me, a foot away, arrow drawn again and, from my eye, foreshortened right to its shaky tip.

"Not. So. Fast."

"I was just—"

"Intruder."

My hands were up, one of them still gripping the hatchet. "We were just taking refuge from the elephant."

"No refugees in my treehouse."

"Don't you think you're being a little extreme?"

"Extremism in defense of liberty is no vice."

I realized that he'd turned my attempted critique into a proud mission statement; I might as well have told Philip Glass he repeats himself.

Goldwater continued: "Hand over the tomahawk."

I lowered it, extended it. I realized that in order to take it from me, he'd have to lower the bow. But what would be my plan then? Take the hatchet back? Attack? Shouldn't I be trying to de-escalate this situation? I'd actually taken a conflict de-escalation workshop once, or rather I was supposed to take one as part of a professional development mandate at an old job, and even though I couldn't recall any of the strategies for de-escalation from the training that I'd failed to attend, I did recall the de-escalation techniques I'd developed in adolescence, and my main strategy was: distraction.

I said, "I was just admiring the weapon. It's beautiful. It looks authentic. Tell me, are you interested in Native culture?"

Goldwater growled, "Hopi. Arizona's just littered with those people, but I like their stuff. Colorful. I collect it. Better me havin' it than them. The warden was kind enough to let me bring some personal effects."

"The warden?"

"Or whatever Coughlin calls himself. Master of some nonsense. He's into all that feudal rhetoric."

"That must have felt nice, to have your needs respected." Reflective listening!

But: "Don't try that shrink crap with me. I have no truck with shrinks."

Two steps to my right was the open door in the floor. My peripheral vision vibrated with it.

I suddenly wasn't sure where Ambrose was, but I didn't want to take my eyes off Goldwater.

"Take it," I said, lifting up the hatchet. "But you'll have to lower the bow first."

"No deal," Goldwater said.

"No," I said, "sorry, I wasn't clear." The hatchet in my hand was feeling heavier now. I was reminded of that old challenge—seen in films of boot camp and fraternity hazings—of holding buckets of water out for long stretches at a time, the moderate weight becoming unbearable when held long enough (weight multiplied by time equaling torture). But I feared that lowering the weapon would signal to Goldwater a retraction of the offer. "I meant that not as some opening salvo in a negotiation. I meant it simply as an observation of physics. You see, to maintain the compressive tension of your weapon, you need both hands, one on the bow, the other on the string and nock. That leaves no hands to accept the hatchet."

"Tomahawk."

"Okay, fine, I just—"

"It's a tomahawk, not a hatchet. Got feathers, don't it!"

"I'm just more comfortable saying 'hatchet.'"

Just at that point, inches from my nose, the only part of the world that was in focus, like my own personal event horizon, I saw the arrowhead—its blade serrated with knicks—shake as he pulled the string farther back.

"Okay, okay! I just meant it as a practical thing. You can't pick this thing up while both your hands are on the bow and arrow."

The senior senator from Arizona considered this. He scrunched up his nose, elevating his thick-rimmed eyeglasses. Then: "Set it on the floor. Then back away."

I exhaled.

He backed up a step and gestured with the arrow to the floor between us.

I lowered a knee to the floor, began to lay down

the tomahawk, when I looked up—had a flash of some sort of Arthurian scene, a knight errant laying Excalibur at the feet of the monarch, the monarch who happened to be shirtless and in some sort of Hopi-drag—and saw Ambrose approaching Goldwater from behind. Ambrose, or rather his silhouette, was holding a large branch. Ambrose brought it crashing down on Goldwater's head. In a moment, Goldwater's eyeglasses hit me in the face, having apparently been knocked right off his face from the blow.

Soon, the two dead men were on the floor, wrestling. Their bodies, all eight combined limbs, which in tangled conflict resembled some sort of humanoid spider in mid seizure, rolled toward the edge of the treehouse.

On my knees, I momentarily excused myself from this scene and tried putting Goldwater's glasses on, expecting some sort of Terminator-like vision, reality red-hued and supplemented by digital grids and crowded by NSA-sourced annotations on the subjects in view, but only finding a world blurred beyond recognition. Through them, I watched a cotton-ball rolling around in the distance until I began to feel nauseous. I took the glasses off, saw reality again in all its hyper-pixelated horror, just in time to see bits of hair-fuzzed scalp that were flying off the fight, which was now getting bitey.

I gripped the tomahawk, pulled myself to my feet.

Approaching the tussle, my eyes were still recovering from my experiment in legal blindness, and the two figures seemed to be superimposed over each other.

They were near the edge. Their bodies crumpled up against the railing with enough tension to push them both up into semi-standing positions, fists circling like atoms around a nucleus.

I fixed my sight on the shirtless one. I lifted the tomahawk with the blunt side toward the two men, blade facing away, and I swung.

In the moment of impact, my eyes closed. The impact itself: absorbed by something both cartilage-y and boney with corners. The heel of my hand met not cold flesh but something more like burlap.

When I opened my eyes, the bottom half of Ambrose's body was slipping over the railing.

I could have run to grab him, but I hesitated, cowed maybe by the rumbling once again of the elephant below. When I finally ran to the railing, and looked down, I saw no Ambrose splayed on the forest floor. He was just gone.

Behind me, I heard a grunting, textured by an emphysemic weeze like scratches on a record.

I turned. Goldwater was on his hands and knees, searching blindly for his glasses. They were just about five feet in front of him, but in between him and the glasses was his bow and a single arrow. He inched forward, his hands sweeping across the wooden floor.

I could run and kick the bow and arrow from his path, but in the time it took me to formulate that thought, his arthritic hand was already closing around the shaft of the arrow.

In a moment, he'd strung the arrow and was pointing it wildly around the treehouse.

He said, "I know you're here somewhere, little mouse."

I had the tomahawk, but even blind he seemed to have the advantage here. And moving toward the door in the floor meant moving obliquely closer to him.

Goldwater said, "I see your strategy there. You were thinking the enemy of my enemy is a friend to me, yes? So you tossed your friend over in the hopes of gaining my trust. I appreciate your strategy, but the enemy of my enemy is still my enemy. Ask Rockefeller, ask Rhodes. Ask all those pussywillows. You're still an intruder, and you're still gonna meet the business end of my flintknap."

He was waving the arrow wildly back and forth now, as I played invisible against the night. I figured in Goldwater's blur, it was movement that would give me away. I wondered if helping him get to his glasses might actually be the safer option here, but then, he found them himself: There was a crunch, and we both looked down. From beneath his wingtips stuck the trifocals. He let out a mournful and pitiable sigh, lowered the arrow, and crouched down to his broken glasses.

I took the opportunity and ran for the door.

"Halt!"

A foot away from the door, I froze.

"Hands up, hippie."

I followed directions. In my right hand, I still had the tomahawk.

"Now turn around. Slowly."

I did as instructed. Goldwater was right in front of me, the arrow, its tension taut, nibbing into my personal space—"my bubble," as my son was taught to call it at daycare. Goldwater had his glasses back on, only the left lens opaque with cracks.

"I'll put the tomahawk down," I said.

"Not so fast, Pippi Longstocking. I'm not falling for that again."

Falling, I thought.

I could hear the creaking strain of the bowstring pulled tighter.

I took a step back, and fell cleanly through the open door.

## SEVEN

I'm not good with free falls. I've always hated roller coasters with vertical drops. Even the little drop at the end of Pirates of The Caribbean has prevented me from returning to that ride. Even when I know I'm safe, the sudden loss of terra firma makes my stomach clench, my lungs seize up, and while others might throw their arms up and whoo all the way down, I struggle just to breathe, white-knuckling the safety bar. Hell, I don't even like Tom Petty's "Free Fallin'," though that might have more to do with its use in the movie *Jerry Maguire*, which introduced me to Petty's ouvre as a soundtrack to sentimental white guy midlife crises, despite Petty's coy tangle of darkness hidden beneath his twelve-string jangle. Sure enough, though, here I was in the midst of my own white guy midlife crisis, suddenly recalling that song; I'd like to think, though, that doing battle with the notable dead of history's patriarchy somehow elevated this beyond the Cameron Crowe brand of noble self-pity. The song was suddenly in my head simply because my body was actually free falling. As the earth was rushing up to me at the acceleration of gravity, the song was blasting its way, with those three gusty open chords, through my head, until the ground would surely and shortly blast its way through my head upon impact. The benefit, I suppose, of this impending impact, would be a simple diagnosis. Since surely the dead could not die, if death was the result, then it would stand to reason that my presence here in this sylvan afterlife was not a mere mixup but in fact a reflection of my actual existential status (that status being: dead). This was perhaps a bit like the bent tautology of drowning a witch to see if she's a witch. This was drowning, this was falling. This was me wondering if I'd be available to FaceTime with my wife and son in the morning, and if so how to explain how I'd spent my evening, in a way that wouldn't seem like I was avoiding the proposed topic of conversation. The day before, my wife had sent me an email mentioning that our son was now old enough to get genetically tested, so we could see what I'd given him, if I'd passed on my gene, the one that had triggered my own cardiac event. As long as we didn't know what sort of life sentence I'd given our son, he would be suspended in some sort of gravity-less state otherwise known as childhood. As far as I was concerned, the job of the parent was to tread gravity while holding up your child, even while your legs gave out beneath you both. My legs, meanwhile, were either above me or below me, depending on your understanding of what was up and what was down. At this particular moment, I was not sure which was what. But here I was, in free fall, a kind of falling people usually seem to find freedom in; I'm thinking of those arms-out videos of sky-divers, Earth's sheer remoteness providing temporary reprieve from the demands of its gravity, the illusion of suspension allowing the fallers a sense of freedom, even while their bodies are at their most vulnerable to Earth's force. This always struck me as strange, this capacity to revel in the illusion of the very freedom that is being denied, and that awareness is surely part of the reason I have never been able to enjoy free falls, but also part of my failure in any number of other endeavors too, such as the purchasing of toothpaste. When Wordsworth wrote that "Nuns fret not in the convent's narrow rooms, / And hobbits are contented with their cells"—or such was my memory of the poem: one cannot consult *Norton's Anthology of English Literature* when rapidly approaching the ground and certain injury—he was attempting to describe the freedom from freedom, from the tyranny of choice, both in terms personal and aesthetic, as for him he flowered "Within the Sonnet's scanty plot of ground," and even though I can find some accord in this latter statement about writing, and can empathize with those

who've felt the incapacitating awe of too much choice—
as my wife described, upon returning from two years
abroad, being struck helpless by the array of choices
in a Bay Area Target's toothpaste aisle, a whole aisle, so
much so that she left without a single minty tube of the
stuff—the specter of someone, especially an authority,
or at least an authorial voice, diagnosing plebeians,
identified only by vocation, as feeling "the weight of too
much liberty," and offering an incarceral prescription
where they "should find brief solace," struck me—even
when I first encountered the sentiment in college—as
essentially the voice of proto-fascism, or perhaps neo-
feudalism, and so perhaps the way my chest squeezes
the breath from my lungs is not only a physiological
reaction to free falls, but an ideological reaction as
well—therefore making my aversion noble rather than a
cowardly refusal to not board the Cyclone—an aversion
so embodied that it—my body—recognizes the free fall
as the ultimate expression of nature's tyrannical bent,
the way it seduces people into the idea that submission
is freedom. Buying toothpaste, though, my strategy is
to grab the first one that catches my eye and dash to the
checkout. Find out later that it tastes like granulated
industrial adhesive. The final thing I did, before leaving
for the artists' retreat and/or tour of the underworld,

was to run to the nearby Target to buy, among other things, toothpaste that was kid-friendly (or at least childish enough in its branding), and the tube that I hastily grabbed—first thought, best thought—turned out, upon my later inspection, to contain a chemical that a study had recently suggested might suppress the liver's production of low density lipoprotein receptors—receptors which I, post heart-attack, learned I was genetically ill-inclined to produce, receptors which the integrity of my heart desperately needed. It didn't matter, I thought, as this was just a kid's toothpaste. But then there was that study. Sure, I told myself, one study—that didn't matter: they don't even bother replicating studies anymore so no one knows anything, and an unreplicated study is just a dream journal of random phenomena. That's what I told myself, that scientific studies these days weren't science, were just spasms of science's epistemological crisis. But then I thought: My son might have my thing, my condition; I can't let him have this toothpaste. And then I thought: But we don't know if he has my condition. And then I thought: But he might. And then I thought: But until we know, he doesn't. And then I thought: Until we know, he does and he doesn't, Schrodinger's heart, suspended. That's the thing about a heart: it can fell a body like a tree but it's powerless against stubbornness; affecting the path of blood through the body is a mere act of plumbing, but altering the neural pathway of my obstinacy would take an act of the supernatural. Still, I returned the toothpaste to Target, only to find that I hadn't kept the receipt, so instead I had to buy a whole new one, while also keeping the old one, which was still sitting in the center console of my car, and which had eyed me on the drive up like a seductive cyanide capsule, the eyes of its off-brand Elmo agog with the death drive—thanatos perhaps being another iteration of the so-called freedom found in submitting to gravity. I wondered if in my free fall I'd reached terminal velocity yet.

I would later learn about the similar fall that befell Ambrose. After I—*accidentally!*—knocked him over the side of Barry Goldwater's treehouse, he passed through the air, atmosphere moving over him in vectors, his mustache fluttering, suit billowing around him, only to land on the leathery back of the passing elephant. His body on the beast was like a string-cut marionette riding a dog. When he gathered himself, the elephant's ears flapping against him like rubber sheets in an automated car wash, he managed to grab hold of one of those ears, saving himself from falling off and into the chaos of the elephant's stampeding feet. He managed to steer the beast—or at least ride it, convincing himself that his perhaps ineffectual tugs on its ears were actually doing something—through the wreckage of the Odin statue, past the mostly melted ice sculpture of Priapus, around the still-smoldering Owl, the embers like a swarm of lightning bugs, and eventually looped back around— as the elephant seemed to be stampeding in ever-widening gyres, if a single elephant can be said to be a stampede—to the site of the treehouse, which Ambrose only knew because suddenly the body of your narrator landed—with the wind knocked out of me so suddenly it sounded like a dry heave—right behind Ambrose.

He was quick to grab my leg and settle me, as much as one could, keep me from falling into the industrial pounding of the elephant's legs. I grabbed hold of Ambrose's torso and held on. Riding bareback on any charging creature puts one's testicles and tailbone in a state of righteous precarity, and my lungs were only now reaching capacity again.

"You saved me," I said. "I would have been ground into the dirt on impact."

"Bah!" Ambrose said. "The drop's but four meters. Five, tops."

We passed a man who appeared to be ironing his toga while it was still on his body.

"Besides," he said, "there's no saving here."

The only reason we were able to hear each other, I suddenly realized, was that our ride had stopped. The elephant had found H.W.'s tabletop, the gin-soaked fruit-flag. The elephant was sucking individual strawberries from the flag's stripes one by one, like a vacuum cleaner finding croutons in couch cushions.

"Dismount!" Ambrose said.

When he swung his left boot over the elephant, his heel struck me in the kidney, which expedited my own dismount.

On the ground, my nostrils were aflair with the loamy funk of the elephant's shit. I looked up and saw it: the act of defecation like an act of creation.

I got to my feet. I was oddly calm. Standing between an elephant inhaling gin-soaked strawberries and Ambrose Bierce, I listened to the gentle thump of my heart. Maybe there was just something calming about watching a one-ton animal eat, but considering recent events, I was doing okay. Focused. I knew what I had to do. Find Father Coughlin, get my leave approved. Return to the land of the mostly living. There was something about the simplicity and clarity of this mission that felt reassuring. Out there, in the living world, objectives were diffuse, maddeningly so. Attempting to walk into the kitchen with the simple goal of getting a bite of day-old pizza was quickly impeded by a kaleidoscope of other minor aspirations—to change out of my jeans and into pajama bottoms, to pee, to see if we still had my copy of *The Hundred Brothers* because I suddenly recalled a phrase that I underlined ten years prior—so much so that I would find myself standing in the middle of the kitchen as if suddenly awakened from a blackout, the clutter of minor desires rendering me oddly desireless. It had occurred to me more than once that my early interest in acting was due in part to the focus on objectives and obstacles. While my grandmother derided my interest in the theater as a need to live in fantasy, she wasn't entirely wrong; it's just that the fantasy was of a life sharpened to the fine pencil-tip of a clear goal, up against an equally articulated obstacle, every moment, every utterance, an unstoppable force colliding with an immovable object, even while my own life felt more like a matrix of idle desires and active shame. Acting, and then—once I realized that real acting required the shuffling of social currency better fitting a croupier—writing, allowed me to pretend I was a person whose whole existence could be forged to one all-defining purpose, like in an old video game, in which the goal was simple: get past the henchmen, defeat the final boss, don't die.

The tomahawk was still, somehow, in my hand.

"A good night for a drunken pachyderm," Ambrose said.

I noticed that the elephant wasn't so much inhaling the fruit bits as bringing them with his trunk up to the mouth he had tucked between his tusks. Its lips curled around each bite.

"So where do I find Coughlin?" I said.

"Told you. Keeps himself in the aviary."

"I mean, where is the aviary?"

Ambrose fluffed his mustache. A twig or two fell free. He looked up, pointed to the stars. "Obey the augury."

The elephant, in his rush to consume the entire fruit-flag platter, clattered his tusks against the wooden table.

Ambrose was pointing. My gaze followed his index, up to the stars. The aggressive smear of them was alarming, overwhelming. It was no wonder that UFO sightings were mainly the mythology of the rural, what with this constant reminder of those other suns, those other worlds.

The wash of stars was darkened here and there by the silhouettes of birds, all flying in the same direction.

"Obey the augury," Ambrose repeated.

"Gotcha."

The elephant looked up, spooked. His tusks were pointing to a dark cluster of redwoods. That's not very specific; after all, we were surrounded by dark clusters of redwoods. But the particular dark arboreal patch that had caught the elephant's attention rustled with quiet activity.

I said, "You see something, boy?" When addressing the elephant, I took on the dopey cadence of a dog-owner.

"Don't trouble yourself with these midnight crepitations," Ambrose said. "More often than not it's nothing more than that Luther Burbank in the thicket, rubbing leaves upon his manhood."

The elephant was not placated.

I looked back to the sky, saw more birds. "Follow them to the aviary, then?"

Just then, a gaunt man in a too-large suit burst into the clearing, directly in the elephant's sights, and ran— all limbs and billowing suit—toward us. The elephant reared up in defense. But in a moment, the man was gone, having dashed right past us, without even a glance at the giant animal he'd spooked.

The elephant clomped his forelegs back down, the

impact vibrating my feet like the first bass note plucked at a death-metal concert.

"Was he obeying the augury too?" I asked.

Ambrose said, "Poor Bobby Oppenheimer. Always the Chicken Little."

Then a corpulent man, nude save for that horse mask, burst out of that same cluster of trees. He was brandishing a whip, and as he ran toward us his belly flopped up and down on his button dick with punishing weight. By now, the elephant was sufficiently on the defensive, so by the time the horse-headed man approached, the elephant kept him at bay with a threatening fanfare.

The man stood there shouting something, but through the horse mask it was all muffles.

"Damn it, Antonin," Ambrose said. "Take that fool thing off if you want to be heard."

The man's posture deflated a bit, but he took off the horse-head. Drops of ice-cold sweat flecked from the rubber mask, a few landing on my face, lips.

While I wiped my mouth on the back of my hand, Ambrose said, "Why don't you leave Bobby be?"

Antonin Scalia threw the mask onto the ground and said, "You can sew that damn mustache to your chin,

Bierce. I'm teaching Doctor Boom-Boom here a thing or two about the universe."

Ambrose said, "With a whip? What kind of lesson did you plan there?"

Scalia looked at the whip in his hand as if he'd forgotten he was holding it. He said, "Bobby Boom-Boom was waxing piteously about Freddie Nietzsche weeping over the whipping of the horse, you know that whole hobby horse, and I told him, 'You're not the philosopher in that analogy—you're the horse, and you deserve a whipping for your insolence. You're built for a job, you do it. You don't do the job, then spend eternity complaining about the world that *you* created!' One must always be an originalist to one's own intentions. Self-examination is the hobgoblin of little minds." He began looping the whip around his forearm, inflated his posture again. He peed a little bit, seemingly unaware, dribblets into the dirt. "Now where's my horse?" He tugged on his testicles. "I'm in the mood to become death and destroy some worlds." He sniffed his palm, seemed to gain strength and energy from the pissy musk.

"I'm afraid I can't aid in your abuses, Your Honor," Ambrose said.

"Harrumph!" This wasn't him clearing his throat; this was Scalia actually saying the word "harrumph." He turned to me, and said, "What about you, shag-bag? Perhaps you can point me to my prey."

I pointed at an angle about ninety degrees off from Oppenheimer's trajectory.

Scalia nodded. "Gratitudes, citizen!" And he ran off.

For such a corpulent man, his backside was surprisingly flat, deflated. Once that bare ass disappeared into the foliage, Ambrose said, "At least they took his gavel away. When all you have is a gavel, everything looks like a nail."

"That a Twain quote?"

For a second, I thought Ambrose was going to punch me, but then he laughed. He had coffin breath.

The elephant swayed his head, a tusk crashing into the nearby redwood. The elephant then gave a solemn honk.

"Mr. Tusk has become crapulent," Ambrose said.

There were a few stripes of strawberries left of the flag.

I had to find the aviary.

Suddenly, a lash was around my neck. And before the whip pulled me to the ground—my esophagus crumpling just a bit—I heard, "You led me astray, shag-bag!"

# Eight.

The tomahawk was still, somehow, in my hand.

I hacked at the ground above my head, hoping to sever the whip that had become my leash. Scalia began dragging me, and my hacking got wilder, more panicked. Stones scraped down my back as he pulled me along. I was making a noise like a balloon just barely pinched shut, the wheeze of my last breath escaping. I felt the blood pooling in my face, the heat and gorge of it.

If my potential for death was a sign of life, then maybe I really was still amongst the living. Maybe this episode of being dragged toward the precipice of death, then, could be brought before the Master of Revels, Father Coughlin, as proof that I did not belong here and must be granted my exit papers. That is, assuming the Honorable Scalia didn't actually send me off that precipice.

I could smell the little air pops of farts, dribbling out of the man dragging me. The farts of the dead have peculiar notes of the petrichoral. Still, my ability to smell was proof of breath, of breathing, like a mirror held beneath my nostrils. Proof that I still had some struggle left in me.

I continued hacking at the whip pulled taut above my head.

When the struggle began to leave my limbs, he stopped. I stopped. The slack loosened. I pulled at the whip around my neck until I could take a full breath again. I coughed into the dirt.

When my eyes cleared, I saw—now through the rose-colored glasses of bloodshot eyes—Scalia standing above me. Having let go of the horse mask and the whip, he seemed unsure what to do with his hands. He touched his belly, fingers moving in little twitches like he was typing.

"Sir," he said, "how do you plead?"

"What?" My voice came out as if through a broken speaker.

"Goddamnit, where's my gavel! I wanna thwap you. I said: How do you *plead*?"

"I'm just trying to get to the Master of Revels."

"Ha! You'll have to get past Cohn first. And that dog of his too. Now: how do you *plead*?"

"I don't even know what—"

"Don't be a fool for Christ! I'm talking procedure, my young defendant, procedure *ipso jure,* so not one more bit of your interpretive jiggery-pokery. Now fess up and cough up a plea, *in haec verba!* Have the courage to suffer the contempt of the sophisticated world! Now a plea, or *in flagrante delicto*, a smack in the face. It's quite easy to determine that smacking someone in the face is permitted in our Constitution, which is *not* a living document. It's dead, dead, dead. And here in the Grove, *sub judice*, we like a little hanky-panky with our dead. After all, sexual orgies eliminate social tensions and ought to be encouraged." He began twisting his scrotum. "Now, it's time for broccoli."

"Oh, God," I said, or thought.

Something splattered on his belly, something red, and for a moment I thought he'd been shot. More red splattered, and some of it, something solid but soft—coagulated chunks of blood from the decomposing viscera of the Justice, maybe—hit my face. A drop landed on my lip: strawberry, with a perfumey patina. Strawberries were bursting from Scalia as if from a pinata. The Justice seemed just as confused as I was. When the next burst of strawberries came, I realized its trajectory was not from him but rather onto him—not *ex*-Scalia but *ad*-Scalia—and I was merely catching the bounce-off.

I took advantage of Scalia's momentary distraction and got to my knees.

To someone behind me, Scalia shouted, "You loggerheaded pettifogger!"

I turned and saw Ambrose, ten feet away, his fist full of more strawberries from the cake, the elephant at his side. He hurled the gin-soaked fruit, mostly making contact with Scalia, but a few hitting me. Ambrose smacked the elephant on his shank. The animal blared and began charging.

I rolled as far out of the way as I could. When I looked up, my corneas dried with dirt, I saw the elephant chasing a surprisingly nimble Scalia into the thicket.

Ambrose helped me to my feet.

"Godspeed, you tusked beast," Ambrose said, staring off into the darkness.

I rubbed my neck, abraded raw by the whip.

I picked up the tomahawk, which was on the ground beside the whip. I grabbed the whip, too, rolled it up around my forearm.

Ambrose said, "He's right, you know."

"About which part? I couldn't understand goddamn most of it. He mentioned something about broccoli."

"About Roy Cohn, and his bulldog."

"Well." Above, the black blurs of more birds, all flocking in the opposite direction the elephant had chased Scalia. "Shouldn't we, you know, obey the augury?"

Ambrose nodded, pointed in that general direction, and we began walking.

He said, "I can't go with you the entire course, I'm afraid. But I suspect you know that."

We were soon into the thick of the forest, and we had to be more careful with our steps, wary of the roots that fingered out from the base of the trees, palming the Earth as if it were a basketball.

I said, "Is that like a jurisdictional thing? Like you don't have clearance into the aviary?"

"It's a teaching-you-to-wipe-your-own-backside thing." He paused, seeming to register the idiom.

Panic bloomed hot in my chest. "But—you brought me here. Shouldn't you—"

He let out a single rhetorical laugh, quite effective in its barkiness. "Reminds me of something my boy said to me once."

Somewhere near, another bonfire was flaring. We were entering its aura of dry, singeing heat. We heard a chorus, voiced more in echo with each other than in sync, chanting, "Boola, boola! Boola, boola!" And then the response somewhere nearer the flames: "Hurl that spheroid down the field and fight! Fight! Fight!"

Then a "hut-hut," then a "hike." Then the sound of bodies colliding, not just colliding: crushing, gnashing, tearing. The snarl of the dead doing *sui generis* violence to each other. Still, thankfully, out of view.

Ambrose and I kept walking, passing obliquely away.

After a moment, during which the light crunch of our footsteps in the underbrush began to be audible again, I said, "Are you saying this is a teachable moment? Christ. And I was starting to like you."

"You really should familiarize yourself with my ouvre before you make characerological presumptions. Just remember to ask your bookseller for the B section, not the T. Got it?"

"T section. Got it."

"Or I could just leave you here. H.W. could use a wheelchair attendant. And I hear he's grabby."

We were nearing voices. We slowed. We heard a "whoop-whoop."

We both stopped. We could make out some movement against the base of a tree.

I clutched the tomahawk, clenched my sphincter.

I began to make out Goldwater, but he was turned away from us, his attention to another man—my vision adjusting—tied to the tree. The bound man said,

"But we're just pretending, Barry. This is all just a fun pretending."

Goldwater said, "I want that scalp."

Reagan screamed, "No, Barry! Just a pretending! Please!"

The *shink* of a knife being unsheathed diced the night.

I yanked on Ambrose's arm and ran. He followed.

We ran until Ambrose's grunts behind me began to take on the quality of little screams.

We caught our breath leaning against the base of a tree gnarled with tentacle-like roots.

Above, the crowding of redwoods was telescoping the navy-blue sky farther away, but I could still see the little blurs of birds heading in the presumed direction of the aviary.

"Your boy?" I asked.

"Pardon?"

"Something your boy said?"

Ambrose gestured for us to keep walking. I followed his lead.

After a few paces, he said, "Said I fathered him, so I should be the one to homicide him."

"What?"

"He had moods. Like wildfire. One day, burned hot

and fast—next, sooty and moribund. One night I was asleep in my chambers. He came to me. Or rather, I opened my eyes and there he was, standing above me. That's when he made the request. I wondered or hoped that he might have been somnambulating, but I knew he wasn't. I told him to go back to bed. He did."

"Manic depressive?"

"Melancholic, maybe, but mostly just a boy. That's what happens when they reach fourteen, fifteen. Next year, he found a woman up in Chico. On the eve of marriage, she decided another man's ring fit a little better, that of his best friend. My boy shot 'em both up, then put the muzzle behind his own ear."

My blood tickenned, and I stumbled over a root. I listened to our footsteps, the white noise of the night getting louder. I began thinking of other things to say; surely we'd be at the aviary soon, but I still felt a panic to make things—something—right. Before I could come up with some abyss-bridging small-talk, he said:

"Can't say I was surprised upon hearing. I had my own flirtations with self-murder. Inheritance is a dimwitted graverobber, rarely lifting the good parts of you."

Soon, after Ambrose told me about his fall from the treehouse and onto the elephant's back, we heard a growling. It was a slobbery sound, jowls flapping wetly. The snarling was soon muted, turned into a chomping. The dog had been given a bone. The grind of teeth punctuating the grunts.

Torchlight licked the edges of trees before us, gave them contours they'd previously lacked, allowed us to see our way cautiously into a clearing.

In an oxblood leather chair sat a hunched man in a baggy suit, legs crossed and body pressed to one side. To his right, a lit tiki torch. To his left, another man, similarly suited but squatting in the dirt. The squatting man had a bone in his mouth, big enough to be a human femur, and he was going at it with insatiable chomps. The squatting man's suit was all undone, untucked, untied, unbuttoned, his slacks split latterly across the crotch, exposing tighty-whities stained off-white. Around this man's neck—this man who was looking down, noshing the bone, his face obscured—was a collar, and buckled to the collar, a leash, the end of which was held by the man lounging in the wingback chair.

The seated man, whose droopy, deep-set eyes sat on dark purple insomniac pillows, gestured to us with his other hand. "Step closer, kitty-cats. Doggy Joe don't bite unless advised to do so."

We did as instructed. When Ambrose and I were about ten feet from them, the seated man raised his palm for us to stop. We did.

Doggy Joe was still enjoying his bone.

"I heard scuttlebutt of this. Ambrose, dear, introduce us to the interloper."

Ambrose put his hand on my shoulder. "He's some sort of writer, Mr. Cohn."

Cohn hid his face in his hand for a second, then reappeared and said, "Oh, not another one of those lookie-loos." He clicked his tongue in disapproval. "You want a scoop, skip on down to the ice cream parlor. You try to scoop anything here, and I'll have Joey use that scoop to melonball your brains out into a nice cut-glass fruit bowl, a Waterford maybe."

"Oh, no, Mr. Cohn," I said. "I'm not a reporter or anything. I'm not here for a story. I'm just looking for the exit, really."

"Not looking for a story, huh?" He made a show of looking himself over, then taking a good long look at Doggy Joe. "Did you hear that, Joe?"

Doggy Joe lifted his head in a jerk. The bone was now in his hands, his chin sopped with drool.

Cohn continued in performative outrage: "Mr. Writer here doesn't think we're interesting enough to be a story. What do you think, Joe, should we try to *interesting* things up for him? Maybe he'd find the junior senator from Wisconsin gnawing his shanks till they're ragged streamers of flesh to be a bit more of a story, huh?"

"No, no, no—" waving my hands as if at an oncoming train.

"Kitty-cat, kitty-cat," Cohn said to me, "relax, I'm only joshing you." He chuckled, a hollow echoey sound. "Jeez, you fright easier than a jumping bean."

Doggy Joe didn't seem to be in on the joke, though. He was eyeing me now, snarling hungrily.

"So," Cohn continued, "if you're not interested in a story, what kind of writer are you?"

I adjusted my shirt, tried to sneak a glance at Ambrose. "Well," I said, recalling some stray sentences from my application to the artists' retreat, "my work attempts to collapse the binary between form and function, interrogating the ways received structures scaffold experience, and what happens when that scaffolding falls—"

"You bore me," Cohn said. "Joe, filibuster!"

Doggy Joe lunged at us, barking to his lungs' capacity. He came within a foot of us when the leash snapped taut. Cohn held him tight. Joe kept barking at us and fighting against the leash. Ambrose and I, somehow, held the space, but I dropped the tomahawk and whip into the dirt.

"Okay," Cohn said, "down, boy."

Joe cocked his head toward Cohn, then slinked back to his side.

Cohn patted Joe on his balding pate. "That's right, you're a big powerful man, Joe. People fear you."

Joe sat at Cohn's feet.

"Now, now," Cohn said. He continued to idly tap his fingers on Joe's forehead, little brow-furrowing taps that the senator absorbed with visible delight. "If you're a storyless scribe, then what brings you to the threshold of the aviary?"

I squinted into the darkness behind Cohn, at first saw no evidence of the aviary, but in a moment my eyes adjusted and some vague latticework began to emerge from the oily darkness. I said, "I'm here by accident."

Cohn gave a hooting laugh. "We all are, kitty-cat. That's the fun of it all. You can only truly enjoy being on top of the meritocracy when you understand it's all arbitrary, all smoke and two-way mirrors."

"No, I mean *here* here. Like, I'm not dead. Not yet."

"Oh, please. You sound like Hoover. Poor sap's been in denial for over half a century."

Ambrose said, "He's right, Mr. Cohn. I'm afraid I brought him through the gates under a misapprehension. Fault was mine, but he's simply looking to see Father Coughlin."

I said, "The Master of Revels, Mr. Cohn. I'm just here to ask to go home."

"Oh, well fetch the ruby fucking slippers, then." Cohn clapped his hands and chuckled. When he realized he was the only one laughing, he stopped and said, "What, seriously? That joke was just sitting there on the table, waiting to be snatched up!"

"Apologies, Mr. Cohn," I said. "I've had a long night."

"All right," Cohn said. "Given your modest and frankly adorable little request, I suppose I can let you pass. Father Coughlin has no pressing appointments that you'd be intruding upon."

I exhaled. Ambrose nudged my elbow.

"Thank you, Mr. Cohn," I said. "Thank you, really."

"Yes, yes," he said. "I'm very generous."

I began to walk forward, when Cohn stopped me: "There is just one thing."

"Yeah?"

"Boss Daddy prefers all visitors leave collateral."

"What do you mean? I don't have anything—"

Cohn whipped the leash, then let it drop, and Joe

leaped. He tackled Ambrose, mauling him. I tried to help, but the scuffle was too frantic. When it finally settled, Joe had Ambrose pinned to the ground, Joe's teeth holding Ambrose's neck. Ambrose lay still.

I approached to help, hesitantly.

"I wouldn't do that, Mr. Writer. If Doggy Joe senses a threat, Doggy Joe finishes his bite."

Cohn waved me over to his perch. I took one step in his direction. Joe was snarling, Ambrose breathing cautiously.

Cohn said, "There's one last piece of business we need to take care of before I can grant you ingress."

I wrung my hands. "Okay?"

"Just in case Boss Daddy does grant you egress from our quaint sylvan retreat here, and just in case you magically become the kind of Mr. Writer who is suddenly interested in a story—" Cohn produced, seemingly from nowhere, a document. With his other hand, he produced from his jacket pocket a pen. He handed me the document, but he kept the pen, slowly clicking it in and out.

The document was about half a dozen pages, secured with a tiny binder clip. The header had that IBM Selectric typeface of legal communique and the blunt formatting of a middle school poem. Across the top: NON-DISCLOSURE AGREEMENT.

"I'm afraid all that you have seen tonight stays with us. Or Mr. Bierce's neck," Cohn sighed, "will return to the death-sharpened teeth of Senator Joseph McCarthy." Cohn shrugged. "And there shall remain in perpetuity."

I was flipping through the document, reading along as Cohn spoke: *Mr. Bierce's neck will return to the death-sharpened teeth of Senator Joseph McCarthy, and there shall remain in perpetuity.* I turned to the front page. My name was right there, middle name included.

"When was this written?"

"We are nothing if not prepared." Cohn seemed to think about that for a moment. "And boozed. We are nothing if not prepared and boozed. Regardless." He held out the pen.

I looked to Ambrose; he was squirming, but not fighting against the teeth-clamp McCarthy had on his neck.

I took the pen, flipped to the last page of the NDA, signed it against my thigh.

As soon as I handed the papers and pen over to Cohn, a rusted gate began to creak open behind him.

I took a few steps toward the sound, and as I passed

Cohn's chair, his hand stopped me with a cold gentle touch on the forearm.

"If you're going to walk into a boss fight," he said, "you'll need something sharper than your wits." He gestured to the tomahawk and whip I'd dropped in the dirt.

I walked over and bent to pick them both up. In doing so, my face came within a foot of Ambrose's. He dared not speak, so as not to start the senator, and his eyes bore something that has remained illegible to me.

(As this little story goes to print, I suspect—with great but not un-weighed remorse—that somewhere Ambrose's neck is returning to the death-sharpened teeth of Senator Joseph McCarthy, and there shall remain in perpetuity, per the NDA. So this, then, as an artifact in the world, is also an apology for the very effect of its existence.)

With the tomahawk in one hand and the whip in the other, I entered the aviary.

# Nine.

As the aviary gate closed behind me, the air took on the red hazy hue of a car's exhaust momentarily illuminated in the glow of a brake light. I coughed. The air had more than the whiff of exhaust—it actually was exhaust. It was a thick, diesel cloud, too dense to see more than ten feet ahead, beyond which the visible world evaporated. Above me, around me, the latticework of the aviary stretched up as tall as the redwoods.

I walked just a few steps, then turned back around, could see the gate but no evidence of any hinges, anything that could allow purchase for manipulation, purchase for escape. I kept going.

Eyes burning in the red smog, I looked around for some sort of path, found twin trenches in the dirt dug by the thin tires of a small car. I walked between them.

Above me, around me, I heard large wings flapping luxuriously, like the sound of someone shaking out a blanket.

"Hello!" I called. "Mr. Coughlin! I mean, Father. Master of Revels, sir!"

The wings were suddenly on top of me. Feathered arms beating at my head. Stronger than I anticipated. The feathers hid sinewy boxer's arms. Above me, the

"

bird's face in profile—a small bald head, beak bulky with a dramatic downturn, all silhouetted black against the red haze: a vulture. That beak began in on my head. Like an ice-pick to the scalp.

I swung the tomahawk above me in a blind fury. The blade didn't connect, but my knuckle caught a claw. As the carrion bird eased off, I helicoptered my arms around. "I'm not dead yet!"

The vulture gave a parting squawk. It ascended, but not too far. Without even looking up, I felt it circling just above me.

I kept walking. The wings above me began to multiply. I was afraid to look up, to see the wake of vultures gathering.

When one squawked, I jumped and dove off the path. In a ditch, my head narrowly missed colliding with the sharp prow of a rock, which offered some coverage, just enough space between it and the mossy earth for a me-size body. I tucked myself in and watched the vultures swoop down and away, carrying off none of my carrion.

I waited. Something wormlike wormed up my leg. Soon, the puttering of a small, un-mufflered engine began rattling the air. My view from beneath the rock was limited, and I didn't want to poke my head out until I could confirm just what the sound was, but I soon found out: Four wheels, thin and spoked, rolled by. The spacing of the wheels seemed too close to be an actual car. After it passed, I peeked out and saw:

A Model-T rattling on down the path, its headlamps clearing the haze before it. Perhaps it was a trick of perspective, but this open-top Model-T seemed abnormally small, the size of a go-kart, just big enough to hold the driver: a figure hunched over the wheel. He wore an old driving helmet, like a leather beanie. And he seemed to be giggling. At first I thought the sound was the puttering of the engine, but it soon became rhythmically distinct, and I could clearly make it out: a constant jittery giggle from the driver.

By now, I was out of my hiding spot, getting to my feet to better see the motorist. He didn't seem to be driving too fast, so I began to follow at a safe distance, knowing he would lead me to Father Coughlin.

As I followed, the giggling never stopped. The rhythm of the giggling and that of the engine had an elliptical relationship with each other, but when they synched up, it seemed as if the motorist were cackling with the force of twenty horsepower.

I needed to cough pretty frequently, due to the exhaust, but did my best to time it with the car's periodic backfires.

The vultures were coming back, gathering one by one, a swirling mass of them just ten feet above my head.

I squeezed the tomahawk in one hand, the whip in the other, reminded myself that I had recourse.

One vulture descended, took a sharp peck at my scalp. I yelped, ducked, and swung. The vulture returned to the swarm, un-hurt if not amused by my attempts at self-defense.

When I got my bearings, I saw the motorist up ahead, his automobile stopped, turned around in his seat and staring right at me. His eyes were obscured by driving goggles, giving his face a bug-like leer. He returned his attention to his steering wheel and shifted gears. Shifting into reverse—a balking sound—he began a three-point U-turn. By the time he'd righted his front wheels in my direction, I'd already bid farewell to my opportunity to escape.

The motorist revved the engine, then accelerated. That little car got larger and larger. A go-kart-size automobile heading straight for you quickly begins to resemble a grown-up-size automobile.

I leapt out of the way, back into the dirt. As the motorist veered by, I heard his giggling intensify into a high-pitched, maniacal laugh.

I got to my feet. I ran.

I ran far enough to wonder just how big this aviary was, then kept running far enough for me to consider that the territory of the aviary was elastic. The tree that I ran face-first into, however, was not elastic; it was quite solid.

This one wasn't the usual redwood, though. It reached into the air with great tentacle branches, an ossified octopus—it was an oak tree. I scrambled up along its lowest branch that curved around like a small road ascending a mountain, until I was able to—after hopping branches—see just far enough to spot the Model-T in the distance, as its headlights softly and sputteringly expanded that distance.

Then I saw it—what the deranged motorist was driving toward. Visible through the haze of exhaust: a monolith. I guessed about two stories tall, arched across the top. The face of it looked meshed, moving as if by breath, with two eyelike knobs at the top.

And that's when I realized that amplified breath was in fact vibrating the atmosphere: "*Shhh phzzphzz phzzshhh* SOMEBODY MUST BE BLAMED *akwjenfaew fakjbfnaiwejfbaw awkurfnawkg* IF JEWS PERSIST *fkgjnekrjgnwe rewrg wekrgjnwejrg wergnerg….*"

That voice, which tore through the static in shards, had a nasally mid-Atlantic honk. It echoed across the aviary as if through Fenway Park.

I was trying to make out the sound of the voice, parse it and its static from the stuttering engine of the Model-T, when I began to hear another engine, quickly approaching from behind.

A small plane flew inches above my head. I lost my grip on the tree. This time, my freefall was swift and brutal. The ground hit my lungs with the force of a baseball bat. Staring dumbly up, I saw the monoplane heading toward the giant radio, which emitted a toxic red glow.

I got to my feet, and as my breath slowly aerated my bronchial tubes again, I followed the path of the plane. I passed through species of flora too colorful to be anything other than invasive, over dirt ribbed with bones, beneath a gathering cloud of raptors heading toward the voice from the monolith.

Approaching, I found cover behind a bush as leafy as a tumbleweed, and I surveyed the scene.

The plane was now flying in loop-de-loops. From the torso of the pilot emerging from between the wings, I could see that this vehicle too was miniature. On the snout of the plane was spray-painted *Spirit of*

*St. Louis.* The pilot, like the motorist, was wearing a leather skull-cap and goggles. The plane's engine noise was punctuated by periodic shrieks from the pilot—random, unprovoked, and serrated. He seemed to be targeting the birds, veering to nab them in the plane's propeller. When he hit one, the explosion of feathers set off another shriek of glee.

The mangled carcass of one bird fell onto the hood of the Model-T, which was doing donuts in the mud, as if in fealty to the great radio that loomed above it, still booming: "*Hakrjbn askdjbfasemn faksjbfasn asdkfjba* AMERICA FIRST *kjbnkjnas asgnasgr asfkjbase* I KNOW THE PULSE OF THE PEOPLE *asdfgsa asgfkuhsd askdubarg lansadfg* IF JEWS PERSIST IN SUPPORTING COMMUNISM *hdgfhdfg....*"

I felt the sharp peck of a beak on my back, claws just below. I screamed, began swatting at the raptor now latched onto my body. By the time I fought the creature back into flight, it had already nibbled at my brainstem a few more times than was strictly needed, and I had stumbled out of my hiding spot, was now squarely in the clearing.

There was a moment when I thought I had not been noticed. But then:

*"Hjksndf* ALIEN *asdjn* ALERT *sdfn* ALIEN *sdf gsf....*"

The sonic impact of the voice hit me in the chest, and I twirled to find another place to hide.

*"Bskhdb kbsg* FORD *sfdg* CHARGE *kjansd....*"

I heard Ford's cackle, and then the rev of the engine. I turned and saw the Model-T's grille growing larger.

The tomahawk was still, somehow, in my hand. My Chekhov's gun, finally ready to go off.

I threw the axe. Fly, tomahawk, fly. Straight to the sticking place, that fucking demon car.

My weapon hit the grille of the quickly approaching car, and bounced off.

"Mother fuck—"

I dove out of the way. As the Model-T veered by, I heard Ford's laughter reach a convulsive state.

In a flash of inspiration, I dashed straight toward the monolith radio. I figured Coughlin's henchmen wouldn't dare risk injury to his edifice, and so if I flattened myself against it I might be able to avoid vehicular assault while making space for an audience with the Master of Revels.

The first part of my plan worked. Having run to the wooden base of the house-size radio, the Model-T and the *Spirit of St. Louis* veered and swooped at me but didn't get close enough to be a threat.

And then:

"*Asdfasg fgh* KEEP AMERICA *nytdsfhgs* SAFE FOR AMERICANS *asdf srgjyt* …."

The sheer vibrational force of that voice blasted my body a dozen feet away. I tumbled into the dirt, into clear aim of Coughlin's henchmen.

When I got to my feet, the violence that the still-rattling speaker was doing to the atmosphere was fizzing my hair.

The Model-T was arranging itself for another charge. I ran in circles—or not quite circles, more like jagged toddler-scribbled shapes—unsure where to find safety. As I heard the vroom of the Model-T's little engine, I also heard:

"*Gadknaw* LINDBERGH *asdf* STRIKE!"

And my attention was pulled up: The *Spirit of St. Louis* was circling, then descending, right toward me.

With the little plane approaching, I flung the end of the whip at it. To my surprise, the whip lashed around the landing gear and, the moment the Model-T was about to flatten me, the plane lifted me into the air. Holding tight to the handle of the whip, I saw the little car pass beneath me.

My moment of parasitic flight did not last long, however, as the plane began to dip. I was unsure if the pilot's screeching was a response to his compromised altitude or just his way of being in the world, but either way, he kept screeching and I was soon returning to Earth. My feet skidded along the dirt until, still holding tight to the whip, I collided with the base of a redwood.

The tree was so gnarled—perhaps from living inside the exhaust-fumed aviary that seemed air-sealed from the world—that its roots were emaciated and curling up from the ground. I hooked my foot into one protruding elbow of a root, keeping me locked to the base of the tree, and pulled on the whip.

Though the diminutive plane offered significant resistance, I now had it under tether. I could exert about as much control over it as I could a kite in chaotic winds, but at least it was something.

Ford was coming at me again, from across the clearing, the giggling getting louder.

Above me, Lindbergh was thrashing around in loops, screeching with every breath.

As Ford approached, I began yanking on the whip in swift jerks. This caused the monoplane to dip in low spastic swoops.

Every second, the Model-T got larger, louder.

I braced one foot against a rock, the other still locked

in the root, and I gave whatever strength I had to one big yank on the whip.

The pitch of Lindbergh's screech spiked, while his plane fell—right into Ford's Model-T.

Theirs was not simply a collision of two tiny vehicles steered by demon ghosts; it was a collision that had serious velocity behind it, a velocity whose trajectory led right to me.

As I dove out of the way of the flaming ball of Model-T and *Spirit of St. Louis*, and as the wreckage became one with the gnarled redwood, I was surprised to find that the cackling and screeching of motorist and pilot, respectively, did not, for one moment, cease.

I got to my knees and ran until I could no longer feel the heat of the fire. At a safe distance, I turned and saw the two titans of industry and influence, still sitting in their respective vehicles, and they appeared to think they were still steering as normal, unaware, it seemed, that they were both mildly aflame and in vehicles wrecked against a redwood.

My palm was chafed raw from the whip.

I approached the monolith.

"*Ajngsd* AMERIC—*jnsgr* RACE *asdknk* USURY *arsegjkan* POWER *hdfgyn*..."

I got close enough to feel my sinuses vibrate.

"*Ehjkrn* AMERICAN CASTRATION *skjng akrgb* THE MAGIC OF *rgfkjalns* A MECCA OR A ROME *askdgjfn...*"

The speaker fizzed with distortion. Standing in the path of the voice felt like standing in a wind tunnel.

"THE COMMON ENEMY *askjdfgn* COMMON BLOOD *sdkfjgna...*"

But I'd seen this before. The Great and Powerful Oz wasn't the ghoulish green face rising from the plumes of flame and bellowing contempt; it was the dotard behind the curtain.

I walked to the edge of the monolith. Once out of the path of the voice, the air felt vacuum-still by contrast.

I peered around the corner. I saw no curtain to draw back. I saw no cowering man in a frumpled suit. I saw only the back of the radio, which featured vacuum tubes, as tall as men and glowing like their spines were on fire. Below that emerged a long chord, thick as an anaconda. The chord concluded in a stout plug, which was stuck in the earth.

"*Sgrwe ltiyhw asg...*"

I walked over to the plug. It was the size of my torso. I looked at the backside of the monolith. I turned back to the plug. I squatted, wrapped my arms around its warm bulk.

I lifted, felt a sudden alarm of pain in my lower back, stopped. I remembered those illustrations on the side of moving boxes: those two contour-line men, with Keith Haring-style proportionality, one lifting a box with his back, a *don't-do-this* line struck through him, beside his double, uncrossed-out, correctly lifting with his legs—a neat little parable, the good twin, the bad twin. I braced myself, did my best to imitate the position of the good twin, and lifted with my legs. The giant plug began to come loose, but slowly, offering a fricative scrape, metal on metal lubricated only with rust.

When I managed to get the thing fully out of its earthly socket, the giant radio went silent and dark. I dropped the plug.

The dark was too dark to be natural. No stars or moon emerged above. After a few moments, my dilated pupils still couldn't make out a single outline of a tree. No evidence even of Ford and Lindbergh's fiery crash.

I held out my hands, moved cautiously. Where I thought I'd dropped the plug, my feet found nothing. I turned, walked, grasping in the dark.

The air seemed clearer now, no longer thick with exhaust, but cool and mentholated in my lungs.

I groped in the darkness until I felt bark, the loose flossy bark of a redwood. I stayed there a moment, holding on to the tree as if to a rock in the middle of a river. And that's when I heard it: the actual river. The light trickle of water.

Above, through crosshatch branches, the navy blue light of dawn was saturating the sky.

I walked toward the sound of the water until my feet felt stone. Before me, light flickered on the rippling water like flashes inside a concussed brain.

I sat on the pebbly bank and watched the water until dawn diluted the night. I began to see the mountains into which we were tucked. Across the river, the bank rose to meet the trees. Behind me, a path wended away. The path looked familiar.

In the distance, I saw the plastic leopard, lion, and she-wolf, now toppled over on their sides.

I figured it was almost time to talk with my wife and son, almost time to choose to know something, about him, about the path of inheritance.

I imagined his little face filling the screen, a blurry moon, always trying to climb into the image.

A turkey vulture landed on a nearby signpost, regarded me briefly with disinterest, flew away. Far up the river, a man was throwing a tennis ball into the water, his dog jumping in to retrieve.

I lifted myself up and found my way back to the path—or at least *a* path, one that might have been a little more obstructed than the alternative but still, ultimately, worked.

## Acknowlededgments

I'm grateful to Diana Thow, Peggy Thow, Anita Allardice, and, for publishing an excerpt of this in *The Santa Monica Review*, Andrew Tonkovich.

Kevin Allardice is the author of three previous novels: *Any Resemblance to Actual Persons* (Counterpoint, 2013), *Family, Genus, Species* (Outpost19, 2017), and *As The Ceiling Flew Away* (Spuyten Duyvil, 2022). He teaches high school in the San Francisco Bay Area where he is a Jack Hazard Fellow with The New Literary Project. He lives with his wife, the translator Diana Thow, and their son.